RECKLESS DEVIL

Sons Of Valentino

Book 4

KYLIE KENT

Ebook: 978-1-922816-42-9
Paperback: 978-1-922816-70-2

Cover illustration by
Sammi Bee Designs

Editing services provided by
Kat Pagan – https://www.facebook.com/PaganProofreading

This book contains scenes of sexual acts and profanity If any of these are triggers for you, you should consider skipping this read.

This is a work of fiction. Names, characters, businesses, places, events, and incidents are either the products of the author's imagination or used in a fictitious manner. Any resemblance to actual persons, living or dead, or actual events is purely coincidental.

Prologue

Katarina

"You'll never amount to anything, girl. You're useless. Absolutely fucking useless," my father yells at me, right before the back of his hand connects with my cheek.

"Ahh, I'm sorry, Dad. I didn't mean it. I'm sorry," I cry. I don't even know what I'm apologizing for. Over the years, I've just learned that it's easier to try to get back into his good graces than it is to argue my innocence.

I'm not sure if it's the apology or my tears that work, but for the first time in all of my sixteen years, my father turns around and walks out the front door of our trailer. I don't move, terrified of what he might do should he change his mind, come back inside, and see I'm not still on the floor where he left me. My fate tonight would be much worse. I lie there and close my eyes, praying I don't hear the unmistakable thumping of his footsteps.

My mom's face appears behind my closed lids, and her voice flits through my mind. *"Get up and run, Katarina. Run and never stop. Get up now!"*

"Shut up," I whisper. How dare she tell me to run. If she thought running was the answer, then why didn't she do it herself? "I hate you for leaving me here," I sob, tears falling down my cheeks. I wish my mother ran, took me away from this man. Away from my own father. Instead, she left without me. And, at this point, I'd prefer to have gone with her. Death would be so much better than this.

My mother was the very definition of a broken woman. I was eight years old when she decided to put an end to her suffering. I was also eight years old when my own suffering truly began. The day my father found my mother in the bathtub, each of her wrists sliced open, blood everywhere... well, that's the day he chose me as his next punching bag. I remember it well. It's hard to forget your father dragging you into the bathroom by the hair, yelling at you and telling you that it's your fault your mother just killed herself.

After all this time, he still reminds me at least once a week that she's gone because I was a useless waste of space she couldn't stomach to be around. For years, I believed him. I truly thought my mother killed herself because of me. I blamed myself, hated myself. And when I was fourteen, I attempted to follow in her footsteps.

I almost succeeded.

I would have... if my best friend Zane hadn't found me and called 9-1-1. He saved my life that day, in more ways than one. It wasn't until I saw the blood running down my arm that what I was doing sank in. And I realized I didn't really want to die. I just wanted to be away from him. I wanted to stop hurting.

Since then, with the help of Zane and the school guidance counselor, I've learned to accept that I wasn't to blame for my mom's suicide. They say no one is to blame, but they're wrong. *He's* to blame, my father, and one day I will make sure he faces the consequences of his actions. At least I like to dream that I'll have the strength, the courage, to overpower him.

But that day is not today. So, instead, I keep my eyes closed and do my best to block out my mom's voice.

"KATY, WAKE UP."

I swat at the hand that's shaking my shoulder. "No, I don't want to."

"Come on, it's serious. You gotta get up, Katy. It's your dad... He's... he's dead." My best friend's words have my eyes snapping open and my body bolting upright.

"What do you mean he's dead, Zane? You can't joke about something like that," I say, leaving off the part about not wanting him to get my hopes up, only to have them deflated when my father walks back into the trailer.

"He's gone, Katy. I'm sorry. His car hit a tree head-on. He's gone," Zane repeats. "He can't ever hurt you again."

I thought relief would wash over me. That hearing those words would finally ease my burden. I thought wrong. Because the only thing I can think of now is *what about me?* What am I supposed to do now?

I'm an orphan. I'm alone.

"Come on. We need to go!" Zane rushes me towards the door.

"What do you mean? Where do we need to go?" I ask, pushing to my knees and watching as Zane packs my backpack with as many of my clothes as he can fit inside.

"We need to get you out of here. You have to hide. I won't let them take you, Katy. I won't."

"Who, Zane? Who's going to take me?"

"Children's services. I'm not letting you go into

the system. You're sixteen, Katy. You have two years before you're an adult. We can hide you for that long. I'll do whatever I have to do. Come on."

I take Zane's hand and follow him out of the trailer. It's not like I have any other options at the moment.

Chapter One

Katarina

Six years later

"Kat, Kat, Kat!" The chants and screams are deafening as I do what I've been trained to do. Smile and wave. Blow a kiss or two here and there but do not engage in conversation.

"Miss Star, how do you feel about singing at the

Giants opening game tonight?" one of the reporters attempts to shove a microphone in my face.

My security is quick to step in and surround me, guiding me into the building. This is the part of my job I'll never get used to, or ever actually enjoy. I love singing. It's the one thing that kept me going through the rough years. The fact that I can make money doing it is a bonus. And not just money, *really good money*.

"Miss Star, welcome to the MetLife Stadium. We're honored to have you here. I'm Kevin Kepler." The older man holds his hand out for me to shake. I look at him. I know from the briefing my team gave me that he's the Giants' manager. He's in a well-fitted suit, his hair just greying on the edges of his face. He's pretty handsome for an older man.

"Thank you, Mr. Kepler, I'm excited to be here," I say as I take his palm.

"Right this way. I'll show you to the dressing room." He releases my hand, turns, and starts walking in the opposite direction.

I have a routine—a very rigid routine—before every show. Even though I'll only be singing the national anthem today, it doesn't matter. I take every single appearance as seriously as if I were performing at the Superbowl Halftime Show. Now that would be an event I'd love to have on my resume. One day, I'll get there. It's close. I can feel it. My last three albums have hit number one worldwide.

"Here you go," Kevin announces, holding open

the door to a generous-size dressing room.

"Thank you so much," I say as I walk inside.

It's nice, especially for a dressing room in a football stadium. I'm still waiting for the day that I get used to luxury. It hasn't happened yet, no matter how many zeros my bank account has or how big of a house I buy. Rooms like this always put me a little on edge. I feel like if I touch a single thing, I'll break it and everyone will know who I really am. An orphaned, trailer park trash girl parading around like some superstar.

I suck in a deep breath, holding it for ten seconds before exhaling. My eyes take in the blue and white themed room.

"I'll leave you to it. See you out there, sweetheart," Kevin says, shutting the door.

I lower myself onto the sofa and pull out my phone. I'm about to call Zane when Hailey, my stylist, snaps her fingers. "Up. We don't have much time, Katy," she says with a French lilt that I suspect is totally fake.

Hailey is a walking billboard for whatever is *in* on the runways in Paris. She keeps her dark locks in a tight, blunt bob. Her lips are always painted with her signature bright-red lipstick, while her face is a flawless porcelain that really doesn't need as much makeup as she tends to use. She is beautiful, on the outside. The inside, well, not so much. She's great at her job, though, which is precisely why I put up with her attitude.

"Ugh, Hailey, I need five minutes. I'm sure five minutes isn't going to make too much of a difference," I plead with her.

"Fine, but if you have to walk out with one eyebrow, it's on you, not me," she huffs as she walks over to the dressing table and begins to unpack her bag of tools. All of which she uses to transform me into the pop star everyone thinks I am.

I raise my brows at Amy and Liam, who just shake their heads while covering their mouths. Amy is my... I'm not really sure what she is. She's everything. I guess you could call her my vice president if I were a business. Which, in most cases, I am. She's also the sweetest person I've met in this industry. I literally stole her from an actor I met on the set of a sitcom. He was being an ass, yelling at her in front of everyone over his coffee being too cold. Well, I walked right up to him and told the ungrateful bastard that she quit. Amy was no longer in his employ, and if he ever disrespected one of my employees again, I would rip his balls off and shove them down his throat for good measure. The cocky asshole laughed me off like I was joking, and I reminded him I hadn't signed up for a comedy. From that day on, Amy has been my number one everything. She's loyal to a tee and my biggest supporter, other than Zane, who I still talk to at least three times a week.

"Go make your call. I'll handle the she-devil," Liam says, as if reading my thoughts.

"Thank you. What would I do without you?" I

kiss him on the cheek before quickly escaping to the other side of the room.

I'm almost ready to hang up when Zane finally answers the call. "Hey, sugarpops, how're things?" he asks in that low, gravelly voice of his.

"Good. You'll never guess where I am right now." I stop myself from squealing.

"Where?"

"With the Giants. As in I'm at the MetLife Stadium. Yours truly is about to sing the national anthem at the start of the game." This time, I let the excitement show in my voice.

"The Giants? And you didn't think to invite me? Here I was, thinking we were friends," he says.

"The best," I assure him.

"Nope, a best friend would have told me they were singing at the fucking Met, Kat. I would have come to see you."

"I know you would. But it's just the national anthem, Zane, not the Grammys." I laugh.

"Does that mean I get to be your date to the Grammys this year?" he's quick to counter.

"Do you even own a suit?"

"No, but I'm sure I could find one for you." I can almost hear his shrug through the receiver.

"Mhmm, and how would your wife feel about you taking another woman on a date?"

"She'd be fine if that other woman is you. Anyone else, and she'd probably cut their head off."

"No doubt. How is Marcia?" I ask. Zane got

married three years ago. Marcia came out of nowhere, and my best friend fell fast and hard.

Their relationship is something I wish I could have. Not that I want my best friend because, well, *ew*. But I do want to be loved, cherished, worshipped. The problem with being me is I don't trust people. I can never tell if someone likes me for me, or for the person I am now. Then there's the fear. What will happen if they find out about my past? I don't really need to wonder too much. I know they'd run as fast as they could, probably right after they sold the story to the tabloids.

"She's good. About ready to pop, I think. How are you doing…? And don't bullshit me, sugarpops," Zane says, breaking through my thoughts.

"I'm good, honestly. I'm about to sing the anthem at a Giants game, and my last album went platinum. What could possibly be wrong?" I ask him.

"Everything. Success, money, fame. That's not what makes you happy, Katarina. You need to find something that does."

"Singing makes me happy."

"Singing, yes. Fame, not so much."

"Every job has its good and bad," I argue.

"Not true. Mine doesn't."

"Zane, you're the president of a one-percenter MC. Your job has way more bad than good."

"That depends on your perspective."

"You know your luck will run out one day. And you're gonna end up behind bars or six feet under."

"Either way, I know you'll come visit me."

"Maybe." I smile, knowing I'll visit him anywhere if he needs me to.

He might be this big, bad, scary biker to most of the world. But to me, he's the one constant who's always been there. Always will be. He's the one person I know I can call if I were ever in trouble and he'd drop everything to help me. Not that I'd ever ask him to do that. Especially now that he has a wife and son, little Declan, with another baby on the way any day now.

"Zane, I gotta go. Talk later. Say hi to Marcia and kiss Declan for me."

"Will do. Go break some hearts with that voice of yours, sugarpops," Zane says.

"I'll do my best." I disconnect the call and make my way over to Hailey.

There are three things I need to do before I go out on stage. The first is to call Zane. The second is listening to the entire *The Eminem Show* album. I know it probably seems like an odd choice, but I don't discriminate when it comes to music. I love all genres, and honestly, the man is a lyrical genius. The third thing I have to cross off my list is a five-minute meditation.

Sitting down in Hailey's chair, I plug my earphones in, hit play on my music app, and close my eyes. While Hailey plasters my face, pulls and tugs at my hair, I block everything out and lose myself to the melody.

Chapter Two

Luca

This is what I've waited for my whole life. It's what's made the grueling hours spent in the gym, the early morning wake-ups, worth it. My first professional football game.

How many people can say they get paid to do what they love? Not many. I honestly thought this would be a pipe dream. How can someone with my last name have... *this?* We're taught from as early as I can remember not to draw unnecessary attention to the family.

Me, being here, entering the public eye... well, I can't see how that doesn't put all of us at risk. I've had many arguments with my pops over it, and I was fully prepared to give it all up. I wouldn't have a problem joining the family business; in fact, I fucking enjoy working for my old man.

The adrenaline, the thrill of the unknown, I fucking live for it. I'd be just as satisfied doing that as I would be playing football. I know my father fought his every natural instinct to keep from pulling strings to get me here. It would have been easy to let him do his thing, get me a free ride, and sign with a pro team. I know a lot of people probably think that's why I'm here. But I don't give two fucks what they think. Because I know how hard I worked to make it, and today I'm going to fucking bask in the success.

Right after I shake this fucking feeling that something's off. That some heavy shit's about to go down. It could be pregame jitters. As I look around the busy locker room, I take note of how everyone's in the zone, hyperfocused, and prepping for the game ahead. It's almost time for us to hit the field for warm-ups. Before I head out to join my teammates, I dig my phone out of my locker. I just can't shake this fucking sense of dread. I hit Romeo's number. If anyone can understand how I'm feeling right now, it's my twin brother.

"Pretty sure you're supposed to be getting ready for a pretty important game, Luc," he answers.

"Yeah, I was born ready for this shit. Is everyone here?" I ask him.

"Yep, waiting for the star of the family to run out onto the field."

"I have a bad feeling, Romeo. Like, something's off," I admit.

"It's probably nerves. Everything's fine." My brother's voice isn't convincing. I know he feels it too. We've always had this weird connection, a sixth sense that tells each of us what's going on with the other.

"Did you bring Matilda?" I ask about my six-month-old niece, Romeo's daughter.

"Of course. She's not missing her uncle's claim to fame."

"I think you should send her and Livvy home. Something isn't right, Romeo." I love all of my nieces and nephews, my sisters-in-law, but I'm particularly close to Romeo's wife, Livvy. We lived together all throughout college—plus it's just really fucking hard not to like her. She's the sweetest, kindest person I've ever met. Other than my mom. How she got involved with my twin, I'll never understand, but their relation-ship works.

"We're in a secluded box with Pops, Theo, Matteo, Uncle Neo, and Aunt Angelica. What the fuck do you think is going to happen?"

He's right. The whole family's there, and fully armed I'm sure. The thing about growing up in the mafia, though, is that you're always walking on eggshells, just waiting for shit to go down.

"I don't know. You're probably right. I gotta go. Just, if anything happens, you get them out of here," I tell him.

"Luca, that's my wife and daughter. You really think I wouldn't get them out at the first sign of trouble?" Romeo grunts, obviously offended.

"I think you'd try to save everyone, Romeo, and I just want you to know... if it did ever come down to it, if you had to choose between me or them, always choose them," I say, knowing full well that's not a choice he ever wants to have to make. This isn't the first time we've talked about it. I've told him I'd choose Matilda over both him and Livvy. Which is exactly what he'd want me to do.

"That will never happen," Romeo growls out.

"Okay, I gotta go."

"Talk to you at halftime," he says, cutting the line.

I MANAGED to get through warm-ups and am now standing in the middle of the field, my hand on my chest, ready for the performer on the platform in front of me to sing "The Star-Spangled Banner." Instead of enjoying the moment, soaking in the fact that I'm about to play my first professional game, I'm scanning the fucking crowd, the stands, the field. Looking for whatever it is that's got me all fucked up.

Romeo insisted it's just pregame jitters. But I know it's not. Something's about to go down. I wish I had been more insistent about him taking Livvy and Matilda home.

The music starts and the opening lines of the anthem float through the air. This has my eyes locked on the singer, Kat *Something*. My sisters-in-law are obsessed with the pop star. I've never really paid much attention to her.

Though she sure as shit has my complete focus now. She sounds like a goddamned angel. A voice straight from the heavens. How have I not heard her sing before? While she has me hypnotized, my eyes drift down her body. And that's when I see it.

A red beam right in the middle of her chest.

Why isn't anyone doing anything? She's surrounded by military personnel, security, and a fuck-ton of other people. *How is no one else seeing this shit?* Without another thought, I run. The crowd turns towards me, the angel on the stage stops singing, and everything goes into slow motion.

Just as I reach her, a sharp pain rips through my side. A pain I fucking know all too well. Something I've experienced before. I've been shot. Again.

I throw myself on top of the singer, my body shielding her smaller frame, and my gaze locks on hers. I can see the shock, the fear in her eyes, and I want to take it away. Tell her that she's going to be okay.

Another bout of pain tears through my nerve

endings as I'm rolled off her. My head drops to the side so that she's the only thing I can see. "In case I die today, you should know you're really fucking beautiful," I tell her.

"Thank you, but you're not dying. I can't live with that kind of guilt, so you'll just have to suck it up and live." She smiles, and I swear I must already be fucking dead, because that is the face of an angel.

Chapter Three

Katarina

Chaos.

I have no idea what's happening right now. It's just utter chaos. People are screaming, running. I'm surrounded by big men. Men who are currently holding me back from getting to the one on the ground. The one who just took a bullet for me.

The man who just saved my life. I need to get to him. I need to make sure he's okay.

"No, let me go. I need to see him. Move." I try to

shove my way through the wall of muscle holding me back. It's no use. I can't budge them.

"I think she wants you to move, assholes." A rough voice overshadows my screams, right before an opening is created. "Need a hand, sweetheart?" A man, the mirror image of the one who landed on top of me, asks as he holds out a palm.

"Thank you," I say, quickly run past him, and drop to my knees next to the guy bleeding on the ground. There are people around him, someone holding a towel to his side in an attempt to stop the bleeding. "I'm Katarina. But you can call me Katy. We didn't get to meet properly."

"Luca." He smiles at me, and I feel butterflies in my stomach. "Do me a favor. Let my brothers get you out of here," he says.

I glance at the other man, the one that looks just like Luca, and then back to him. Of course it's his brother. They're identical. "Are you going to be okay? Why isn't there an ambulance here yet?" I yell out, scanning the stadium while wondering what's taking them so long. There are medics hovering beside us but I don't see an ambulance.

Shouldn't they be taking him to a hospital? Why are they just standing around?

"I'm fine. This is nothing. Just a scratch." Luca smirks.

"Come on, let's go."

I'm pulled up to my feet by his brother. I'm about to argue, to tell him to let me go. That I don't want to leave without knowing that Luca will be okay.

"Romeo…" Luca says, his eyes flicking between me and his twin.

"I know, man. I know," his brother sighs.

What does he know?

My eyebrows scrunch down in confusion. "No, I need to stay here," I tell them, when *Romeo* starts to lead me away with his arm around my shoulder.

"He's going to be fine. Trust me. I wouldn't be leaving his side if I thought otherwise," his brother says.

"No, I should stay. This is my fault." I shake my head.

"No, it's not. Luca wants me to get you out of here, and that's what you need to do. He won't relax and let them help him properly until he knows you're safe."

I drop my eyes to Luca, and he gives me a silent nod. "Okay, but I want you to bring me to whatever hospital they're taking him to."

"I'm Romeo, by the way." His brother smiles down at me as he escorts me off the field.

"Katarina," I say, introducing myself.

"I know who you are. My wife and daughter are huge fans." He laughs.

"Oh." I never really know how to respond to people when they say that. Don't get me wrong, I'm thankful to my fans. If it weren't for them, I wouldn't be who I am today. I wouldn't be Kat Star, the latest pop sensation—that's what the tabloids call me anyway. I'd still be Katarina, the orphaned girl living off the streets. I follow Romeo to an underground parking lot that I didn't know existed. "Wait, my team…" I drag my feet till we come to a halt. "I can't leave them…"

"Sweetheart, it wasn't your team who had a red dot painted on their chests. That was you. The bullet my brother just took was meant for you. I don't think you understand the severity of the situation here," he tells me.

"I understand just fine. But they're my employees, my friends. I can't leave them behind just to save myself," I say more firmly.

"Where'd you leave them? I'll have one of the boys go and collect them," he offers.

"What do you mean one of the boys? Who is one of the boys?"

"Friends, family, whoever is available." He shrugs.

"They were in the dressing room. I haven't seen any of them since I walked out."

"Who are we looking for? I need names, sweetheart."

"Hailey, Amy, and Liam," I answer him.

"And who the fuck is Liam?" Romeo says the name on a growl.

"My manager." My eyebrows draw down. I have no idea what's shifted his mood all of a sudden.

"I'll make sure they get out of here safely. Come

on, get in. We need to go," he says, pulling his phone out of his pocket.

I don't know why I do it, but I take him for his word and climb into the car. I mean, if I can't trust the brother of the man who just risked his life for me, who *can* I trust?

AFTER AROUND THIRTY minutes of driving, Romeo pulls into another underground garage. "Where are we?" I ask, looking around. I don't have my phone, my bag, anything.

"My place," he says, switching off the ignition.

"What? No, you said you'd take me to the hospital," I argue. Yanking my door open, I jump down from the huge SUV and spin in a circle in search of the closest exit.

How could I be so stupid? I know better than to blindly trust a stranger. This is a setup and now I'm trapped. I need to find a way out of here.

"Katarina, relax. I'll take you to the hospital. I swear. I just need to get my wife and daughter first. Because if I don't, Livvy will have my fucking balls in a jar on the mantle."

"Livvy?" I question.

"My wife. Come on."

And once again, I'm forced to question my sanity as I follow this man to God only knows where. "Just so you know, people will be looking for me. If I go missing, it'll be front-page news."

"Duly noted." He laughs.

The elevator opens onto an expansive foyer, and just as I'm taking in the over-the-top, luxe surroundings, a woman's scream echoes off the walls. "Romeo Valentino, I swear to God if you're not already dead, I'm going to freaking kill you. You just took twenty years off my damn life." A petite, strawberry blonde appears in front of us with a baby in her arms.

"Liv, babe, I'm fine," Romeo says, embracing who I'd take an educated guess is his wife. "How you doing?" he asks the woman before placing a kiss on her forehead.

And here I am, a stranger amongst them, looking in on an intimate moment I shouldn't be privy to. Neither of them seem to care though.

"I'm fine. We're fine. How's Luca? Where is he?" the woman questions, pulling back to look up at her husband.

"He's on his way to Regional. He's fine," Romeo says.

"Why are you here? We should be there. We should…" his wife says, stopping her sentence when she notices me. "Ah, Romeo, that's Kat Star. As in *the* Kat Star. She's in our apartment," she whispers.

"I know. I brought her here." He smirks, taking the baby from her arms.

"Katarina, this is my wife, Livvy. And our daughter, Matilda." Romeo motions to the two.

"Hi." I wave shyly. I have no idea what to say.

"Oh my god. I'm so sorry. I didn't see you there. Come inside. Are you hungry? Thirsty? Can I get you anything?" Her words come out in a rush of questions.

"Ah, no, I'm good. Thank you," I say.

A man walks into the foyer, stopping short when he sees me. "Um, Romeo, I'm heading out. You got this?" he asks, without taking his eyes off me.

"Yeah, Zio Neo, this is Katarina. The girl Luca just saved from having that bullet rip through her chest," Romeo says.

"Romeo, you could warn a girl before you bring home a star." A beautiful woman with long dark hair barges past the two men. "Hi, I'm Angelica. It's an honor to meet you," she says, holding a hand out to me.

I grasp her palm and shake it with a smile. "Hi, I'm sorry about what happened… to your…" Well, I don't know how they're related. I can only assume that they are.

"Don't be. That kid's been catching bullets just as long as he has a football. He'll be fine." She smiles and then turns around. "We're going to your parents' house. Call your mother, Romeo, before she kills us all."

"Right, I will. We're heading to the hospital now," Romeo says and I audibly sigh.

That's the only place I want to be right now. The hospital. I need to see for myself that Luca is okay. I know his family all seems to think he'll be fine, but the man was shot. People don't just get shot every day. Although, judging by the reactions of my present company, you'd think it was a normal occurrence.

And then Angelica's words replay in my mind. *That kid's been catching bullets just as long as he has a football.* What does that even mean?

Chapter Four

Luca

Beep, beep, beep.

The sound that breaks through my subconscious isn't unfamiliar; it's also not the least bit comforting. Prying one eye open, I'm met with the white of a ceiling. So I turn my head and see the machine that's currently creating that annoying fucking sound. The scent of antiseptic fills my nostrils as I inhale, and pain fires down the right side of my body.

"Fuck!" I groan out as I pull myself upright.

"Shit, no. You're not supposed to move. Lie back down."

I'm stunned motionless by the vision that comes into my view. My eyes flick around the room. I'm definitely in a hospital. "Huh, I thought heaven would have nicer furnishings," I mutter.

"What?" The bellezza in front of me scrunches up her face.

"Heaven, I thought it'd be nicer."

"You're not in heaven, Luca. You're in the hospital," she says.

"No, you're wrong. A bellezza like you would not be here unless I was already dead."

"A what?"

"Bellezza, beauty." I translate the Italian word that fits her perfectly.

"Ah, thank you? But trust me, this is a hospital, not heaven," she reiterates. "And you really should lie down. You were shot. You need to rest."

"No, what I need to do is get out of this fucking bed." I pull at the cords attached to my body, just as the door to the room flies open.

"Luca Valentino, don't even think about getting out of that bed. Lay your ass down, right now," my mother practically yells at me.

"Ma, I'm fine," I argue weakly as I do exactly as I'm told. Because, well, she has *that* tone. The mom voice. And Katarina's lips lift up at the sides like she's trying to hide a smile. "Don't let the nice and innocent look fool you, bellezza. She's the scariest one of us all. *And* she's Australian," I tell her with wide eyes.

"Um…" Katarina says, glancing between me and my mom. "I can go and give you guys some space. I just wanted to make sure you were okay. I don't even know how to thank you for what you did for me."

"You don't need to leave. Stay… please," I practically beg her.

"Hi, I'm so sorry I didn't introduce myself. I'm Holly. It's lovely to meet you." My mom eyes us with a barely hidden excitement on her face. And I know exactly what she's thinking. The woman has been nagging me to follow in all of my brothers' footsteps and find a nice girl to settle down with, so she can plan another wedding.

"Hi, I'm Katarina. It's so nice to meet you and I'm extremely sorry for this."

"This isn't your fault, sweetheart, and Luca's going to be fine. Don't worry about it," Mom says, and rambles on about one thing or the next. It's what she does when she's nervous or anxious. Me, being laid up in a hospital bed, has her on edge. A lot more than she's showing right now.

"Ma, where's Pops?" I ask, to stop her from saying more than she should. Like bringing up how she wants more grandchildren.

"He's on his way up. He was talking to your brothers out in the corridor," she replies, squeezing my hand.

"They're all here?" I groan.

"You were shot, Luca, *again*. Where else would everyone be?" Mom scolds.

"Is there morphine in any of these tubes?" I look around for a dosage button.

"Why? Are you in pain? Sorry... stupid question. You were shot. Of course you're in pain," Katarina huffs out.

"Stop. I'm fine. Really, I'd just prefer to knock myself out before that door opens and everyone bursts in," I say, grasping her palm and giving it a reassuring squeeze. I glance down. I like how her hand feels in mine. Hers is small, her skin silky soft. While mine looks monstrous, huge in comparison. I'm lost in my head and sorting through why I like the feel of our conjoined hands when the door flies open.

Katarina pulls away and takes a step back as everyone, and I do mean everyone, piles into the room. I lock eyes with her, trying to tell her without words not to leave. I can see it on her face. She's uncomfortable being here. I don't like that look on her. I want her here. I'm not entirely sure why just yet, but I'll figure it out. Everyone is talking loud, fast. I can't keep up with anything any of them are actually saying.

"Tranquillo." My father's voice booms over the white noise. They all stop at once and I swear you could hear a pin drop. My old man is the boss of our organization, family, whatever you want to call it. So when he speaks, you listen. "How are you, son?" He looks directly at me.

I shrug a shoulder, wincing at the pain that tears through my side with the slight movement. "I've been better," I say.

"You've looked better too." My older brother, Matteo, laughs. "When you gonna learn to dodge a bullet properly?" he adds.

"Tao, stop messing with the poor kid. Luca, are you okay? Do you need anything?" Savannah, Matteo's wife, says.

"I'm good. Thanks, sis." I give her a reassuring smile.

Savvy's been Matteo's best friend as far back as I can remember. She's always been there. The girl's like a sister to me. But she became family when she and Matteo decided to run off and get married one drunken night in Vegas.

"Where are the kids?" I ask her.

"At home with Izzy. We're all praying they aren't traumatized after being left in her care," she jokes.

Izzy is my cousin, my Zio Neo and Zia Angelica's daughter. To say she's a little unhinged would be putting it mildly. But she'd do anything to protect any one of us. She may be scary to those outside the family. But to us, she's just... Izzy.

"You know, if you wanted to be a hero, you should have joined the military. Catching bullets at a football game is not the way to go about it." This comes from Theo, who proceeds to smirk at his own lame dad joke.

He's the oldest of us four boys. He's also the family's underboss, preparing for the day he takes Pops's place. His wife, Maddie, has a twisted family history. Her mother was best friends with my father and uncle until she ran off and married a Russian. And let's just say neither side took the news too well.

However, it was the Russians who ended up killing Maddie's parents, leaving her to care for her sister. When we first met Maddie and Lilah four years ago, they didn't know much about their lineage, just what little information their mother chose to share. Lilah was only sixteen and sick. She was in need of a transplant, and when it turned out that I was a near perfect match, I didn't think twice about giving up one of my kidneys. I know people think our friendship is odd. I mean, it's not normal for a guy like me to befriend a young, sick girl. But there's something about Lilah that drew me to her. She's a fighter, stronger than most made men I've met. But she's also one of the most loyal and honest people I know.

After the transplant, Lilah made a full recovery and has been well ever since. She's even on her way to completing her medical degree at a college in the city. Theo and Maddie continue to make her get checkups all the time. Both of them are terrified her body will eventually reject the transplant.

"Where's Lilah?" I ask them. Of all people, I thought she'd be here.

"I'm here! Sorry. Traffic was a bitch," she says, pushing her way into the room.

"Lilah, language," Maddie scolds her.

"Sorry." Lilah winks at me as she apologizes to her sister. "How are you? Because if you need this kidney back, it came with a no returns policy. Just sayin'." She laughs.

"It's all yours. Trust me, I put that thing through years of abuse before I gave it to you. It's not as great as you might think." I start to chuckle and immediately stop. Movement from someone I've been watching out of the corner of my eye has my head snapping in her direction. "Katarina, come and meet…"

"Oh my fucking god! Kat Star. Luca, that's fucking Kat Star. In your hospital room!" Lilah screams at the top of her lungs.

"Yeah, and if you'd at least pretend to play it cool, I was about to introduce you to her," I tell Lilah. "I'm sorry. You'll have to excuse my niece, Katy. Her guardians refuse to send her to decorum school. They opted for medical school instead." I shake my head, like it's Theo and Maddie's fault that Lilah doesn't have an ounce of cool.

"It's okay. Hi, it's a pleasure to meet you, Lilah."

"No way, the pleasure is all mine. And ignore Luca. Also, not his niece. I'm his brother's sister-in-law. It's complicated and really not all that important because you're Kat fucking Star." Lilah is jumping on the spot, her eyes bugged out with her obvious excitement.

"Language!" Both Theo and Maddie say at the same time.

34

"Shit, sorry." Lilah turns and looks at Livvy and Romeo right as he pretends to cover Matilda's head.

"Wait. Bring her here." I point to my niece.

"Ah, Luca, you can't hold her. You have stitches," Livvy whispers, like it's a secret.

"Olivia Valentino, that is my niece. If I want to hold her, I can and I will. Besides, what better medicine is there than getting cuddles and kisses from one of my favorite girls?" I smirk.

Romeo plucks Matilda from Livvy's arms and brings her over to me. "Be as rough as you can be, Tilly," he says to the baby before placing her on my chest.

"Katy, this is Matilda. She's a huge fan too. She's just way cooler about it than that one over there." I gesture to Lilah, who's still frozen in awe.

"Okay, since you're breathing and appear to have a heartbeat, I've got shit to do. I'll be back later," Theo interjects. "Lilah, we'll give you a ride back to campus," he adds quickly.

"Sure, thanks. Okay, call me if you need anything, unless it's a kidney," Lilah replies, staring long and hard at Katarina for a minute before she follows Theo and Maddie out of the room.

Chapter Five

Katarina

I've felt like an imposter most moments throughout my life, but never as much as I do right now. In a room full of strangers.

"I, ah, I need to go. But again, thank you. For everything," I say to Luca, who is busy getting covered in smooches from his adorable little niece.

His head turns sharply in my direction. "Where are you going?" he asks.

"Home," I tell him.

"No."

"What?" *What does he mean no?*

"Katarina, you have someone actively trying to kill you. You're not going home without any kind of protection," he says matter-of-factly, as if he's in control of my actions.

"Actually, I can and I am. I don't mean to be rude. I really am thankful for what you did and all, but I'm not going to stop living my life because some deranged fan thinks my death will be their claim to fame or whatever." I turn and storm out the door. I don't look back, even when I hear a hissed "fuck!" try to follow me.

"Luca, sit down," his mother says just as the door slams shut.

Leaning against the wall just outside of his room, I close my eyes and breathe in. I have no idea why it's so hard to walk away. I don't understand this pull he has on me. The door swings open again, and just as I open my eyes, a pissed-off and pained Luca stands mere inches in front of me.

"What on earth are you doing?" I gasp, running my eyes up and down the length of him. He's wearing a hospital gown, with one hand clutching his side.

"If you're so insistent on going home, then I'm coming with you. I didn't just get lead pumped into me to stand by and watch you be reckless, bellezza," he grunts.

"You're insane. Get back in there on that bed." I point to his room.

"I will, right after you," he counters.

"Are you high?" I ask. "And why isn't anyone doing something?" My eyes flick from side to side along the deserted hallway. "You need to be lying down, damn it." My hands wave around erratically.

"Because no one can change my mind. If you want to go home, that's fine. I'll take you."

"No. You really need to go rest, please." My voice is lower. A plea.

"Come with me. I promise my crazy family will be gone soon. Just come back in there with me."

"You don't even know me, and from the limited experience you've had, it's actually a threat to your life to be around me. So, why? Why do you want me to hang around in your room?"

"I want—no, I need to know that you're safe. That all of *this* wasn't for nothing. I'm not a fucking hero, bellezza. I don't go around jumping in front of bullets for just anyone."

"Why me?"

"I don't know. You're different."

"Different good or different bad?" I press him.

"I'm not sure yet, but if you leave now, we may never know," he says.

"Argh, fine. Come on, let's go. You need to get back on that bed," I tell him.

"Thank you."

I don't say anything as I hold the door open for him to walk past me. When he does, I get way more than I bargained for as my gaze lands on his bare ass through the opening of the hospital gown. My eyes widen and my face heats when he turns his head around and catches me staring at his ass. He smirks— a smirk I'm sure has melted the panties off plenty of women.

"For the love of God, Luca, if you don't get back in that bed, I'm going to handcuff you to it," his mother says. "T, tell him he has to stay in bed. He has a bullet wound."

"Dolcezza, he's fine. Luca, stay in the fucking bed. At least till we're gone," his father adds.

Luca's twin helps him climb back on the bed. "So, what's it like?" Romeo says.

"What's what like?" Luca questions.

"Having no control over the one thing you want to lock away from the rest of the world?"

"Fuck you," Luca replies.

"Right, Romeo, I need to get Matilda into bed. You stay here. I'll go to your parents' house for the night," Livvy says.

"It's about time. Tilly's been asking for a sleepover with Nonno." His dad takes the baby out of Livvy's hands.

This family is something else. I'm nothing more than an outsider looking in. But they're so openly loving with each other; the connections they have are so deep. Or at least they appear to be. I learned a really long time ago that things aren't always how they seem.

"I'll be back in the morning. Are you sure you

wouldn't rather come home? T, maybe we should just have Doc stay at the house," his mother says.

"He'll be fine, Ma. I won't leave his side," Romeo promises her.

"Okay, well, call if you need anything." Their mother kisses Luca's cheek, wiping a stray tear from her face. "You really need to stop doing this to me, Luca. I'm gonna go grey." She smiles, but it's not the happy kind.

"Ma, you're a redhead. Redheads don't go grey. They go white," Luca reminds her with a smirk.

"Not the point. I love you."

"Love you too, Ma," he responds.

All my life, I've wished for something like this. What he has. Parents, siblings, a family who loves him. I'll never have that. I'm only fooling myself to think I will. Zane is the only family I have. He and his little family are all I need.

"Right, let's go. I've got Tom and Joey outside. No one's getting in here who isn't on the list," his dad says before leaning down and kissing Luca on both cheeks. Again, I watch in awe.

"Thanks, Pops."

"I'll be back in the morning," Mr. Valentino says as he leads his wife and daughter-in-law out of the room.

"Oh, wait." Luca's mom stops and pivots on her heel. She walks up and wraps her arms around me. "Thank you for coming back. I really hope I see you again soon, sweetheart."

Her words are whispered into my ear. And I have no idea what to say in response. I'm so shocked by her hug it takes me a moment to remember my manners and return it. "Um, it was nice meeting you, Mrs. Valentino."

"Holly. Just Holly is fine."

"Holly," I repeat.

MY EYES POP open with the sense of being watched. I jump up and take in my surroundings. It's when my gaze comes back around and lands on a pair of dark brown irises that I know why I had that feeling. I *was* being watched. By him. Luca is sitting upright in the hospital bed, his eyes boring into mine.

"What time is it?" I ask him.

"A little after two a.m."

"Why didn't you wake me? I'm sorry I fell asleep." I wipe at my mouth, hoping to God I didn't drool everywhere. Thankfully my lips are dry and not covered in slobber.

"You looked too peaceful to wake," he says with a half shrug.

"Where's Romeo?"

"He went to get some food." Luca shifts over to the edge of his bed and pats the empty space. "Come here."

"I-I can't," I say.

"Why?"

"Because... I don't know. I might hurt you...?" I question.

"You won't. Come on. You're tired, and it's my fault you're still here. So please lie down, and I promise I will do my best to keep my hands to myself." He lifts his palms in a placating gesture.

"I feel bad," I say, slowly making my way over to him.

"I feel bad that I forced you to stay," he counters.

"I can go. You should probably be sleeping anyway."

"I want you to stay, even if I do feel like shit for causing you shitty sleep."

"I've slept in worse places than a hospital chair." I shrug.

A dark look crosses his features. "Like where?" he asks.

"You don't want to know." I avoid talking about my past.

"I wouldn't have asked if I didn't want to know," he urges me.

"Okay, well, I don't want to tell you then." I smile as I climb onto the bed and rest my head on his pillow. I close my eyes and take a deep breath. And I'm immediately assaulted by his scent. It's all woodsy and mint. And something else. I can smell a faint hint of... whiskey? My eyes pop open. "Have you been drinking?"

"No, why?"

"I can smell whiskey," I say.

"That's Romeo. He was drinking in here. I don't drink anymore, one kidney and all that." He shrugs.

"What was all that kidney talk about anyway?" I ask him.

"When Theo met his wife about four years ago, her sister was sick. Lilah was on the wait list for a transplant. I was a match so I gave her one of mine."

"You just gave someone a kidney? Someone you didn't even know?"

"Yeah, she needed one. I had two. So why not?"

"I thought you said you weren't a hero." I use his own words against him.

He laughs a little, then stops. "Trust me, I've done more bad than good in life."

"We've all done bad, but not everyone can say they've saved lives."

"I think you're sleep-deprived, bellezza. Close your eyes and try to rest."

"I will if you do too," I tell him.

"Deal," he says, running his fingers through my hair. It's nice. I should stop him, but I've never been good at doing what I should. Instead, I curl into his side more and fall asleep to the feel of him combing a hand through my hair.

Chapter Six

Luca

"Shh, don't fucking wake her up," I hiss at Romeo, who's just reentered my room.

"When did this little development happen? Do we need to have the birds and the bees talk, bro?" He lifts one eyebrow at me. Which I find funny, considering out of all my siblings, I'm the only one *not* reproducing.

"Don't be an ass. What'd you find out?"

"Not much. I've got Christian digging further.

Though it'd really help to actually ask her if she's had any death threats or anything."

"I'm not fucking asking her that," I tell him between clenched teeth.

"Asking me what?" A sleepy Katarina sits upright, blinking a few times before turning her gaze from me to my brother.

"Nothing, bellezza. Romeo was just saying how Matilda loves dancing to your songs."

"Oh, that's cute," Katarina says. "What is it that you want to ask me and he doesn't?" She narrows her glare at Romeo this time.

"Ah, this is not my fight. You'll have to get that out of him." My brother holds his hands up in a mock surrender, and Katarina looks at me expectantly, her eyes wide and her brows raised.

"You know what? I have enough people who like to bullshit and fluff about truths in my life, so if you don't want to tell me what you're too afraid to ask, then I'll just be leaving now."

She moves to get off the bed. Reaching out a hand, I grab her wrist lightly. "He wanted to ask you if you've had any death threats before? If there is anything you can tell us that would help find the asshole who tried to shoot you yesterday?"

"Well, yeah, but mostly I just hand them over to security or police if they're really bad." Katarina shrugs.

"*Them*? As in more than one?" I attempt to clarify, my body tense as fuck.

"I get a lot of fan mail, and I like to answer all of it myself. So a couple of days a week, I open mail and, well, some of it's not as nice as others," she explains.

"Where do you keep all this mail?" Romeo asks her.

"At my house."

"Okay, let's go. I'm gonna need to see it," he says.

"Wait... what makes you think you guys can figure out who this person is when the police can't even find them?"

"We're smarter, and much more resourceful. Also, we're more invested in keeping you safe than the police ever will be," I answer her, then turn to Romeo. "I need clothes."

"Here." He drops a bag on the bed.

"Thanks." Sliding down, I pull a pair of jeans out and slowly manage to guide them up my legs.

"What are you doing? I don't think you should be up yet? Isn't there a doctor or a nurse or someone who actually works in this hospital around?"

"The doc came in while you were sleeping and said I could go home."

"Why do I find that hard to believe?" she questions me, though I suspect it's supposed to be rhetorical.

"You can read the discharge papers, babe. He signed on the dotted line," I offer, pointing to the clipboard hanging off the end of the bed. I slip the hospital gown off and toss it on the floor before digging through the bag for a shirt. I pull out a black

V-neck, wincing only slightly as I put my arms through the sleeves and then yank the shirt over my head. When I'm done, my eyes land on Katarina's again. She's staring at me, her mouth hanging open. "What?" I ask.

"Ah… nothing." She shakes her head, and I can't help the smirk on my face. I've seen that look a million times before. Only this time I'm actually enjoying it. It's a look of appreciation, of hunger, at the sight of me. I might sound conceited, but I fucking work hard for this body.

"When you're done, I do have a life that revolves around more than babysitting your ugly ass. Get a move on," Romeo grunts.

"You do know we're identical twins. If I'm ugly, what's that make you?" I ask him as I retrieve a pair of Louboutin sneakers from the bag. I drop the shoes on the floor and look at them. There's no way I'm bending down to slide my feet into those.

"The good-looking one, obviously. It's a known fact that every set of twins has an ugly duckling. And I'm sorry to say it's you, bro," Romeo says as he bends down and picks up a sneaker, holding it open so I can slide my foot inside. He thinks he's being original, but really he's just repeating our older brother's favorite saying—Matteo insists he's God's gift to women and the rest of us may as well be mutants. Though, I guess now that he's married, he's God's gift to one woman in particular. Savvy owns that man, heart and soul.

The thing about us, as much shit as we give each

other, I'd doubt you'd ever find siblings closer than we are. The fact that he helps me put my shoes on when I can't bend down to do it myself says a lot. I know he'd do it for our other brothers, he'd just make them actually ask for help first, knowing full well they'd both fucking hate looking like they couldn't do something.

"Thanks," I say when he straightens back up.

"I'm driving. I don't need you passing out from blood loss," Romeo says, walking out of the room.

I pick up the bag. It's fucking Louis Vuitton and I'm not about to leave it behind. When I get around to the other side of the bed, where Katarina is now standing, she snatches the bag out of my hand. "He's joking, right? You're not at risk of bleeding out, are you?" she asks.

"No, I'm fine. Come on, let's go hunt down whoever the fuck thinks they can try to take you out," I tell her, waiting for her to walk in front of me.

"Has anyone ever told you you're bossy?" She glares at me from over her shoulder.

"Never," I deadpan.

"Huh, well, I guess all your friends are either too stupid to notice or too scared to tell you."

"Probably the latter."

It takes longer than it should to reach the front of the hospital. By the time we do, Romeo has an SUV parked and waiting for us.

"Do you know you have two dudes in black suits following you?" Katarina whispers to me.

I glance behind me. I knew Joey and Tom were tailing us. "They're family," I say.

"How big is your family? Those guys look like they're straight out of *The Godfather*." She laughs.

I look at her, really look. I've never considered opening up to anyone about what my family does, who we are. I'm not about to let Katarina know either. Well, not just yet anyway. I'm not a fucking idiot. The safety of my family is worth everything, and talking to the wrong person can cost any one of us our freedom, our lives, or both. I won't risk my family because I'm... smitten? Infatuated? I don't know what I am. But whatever it is, I know I can't tell her that they look like the mafia because we're *it*. We're not just part of the mob; we're at the top.

Opening the back door, I wait for Katarina to climb into the car. "Wait... you're not actually the mafia, are you?" she whispers.

"That would be absurd, right? Babe, have you ever actually met anyone from the mafia before?"

"Well, no. But I guess if I did, I probably wouldn't know, would I?"

"Probably not," I agree, shutting the door and gingerly climbing into the front passenger seat.

"You good?" Romeo asks me.

"Yep," I say, my voice tight, the pain almost unbearable.

"Want something?" he offers.

"Nah, I'm good." I grit my teeth as he pulls away from the hospital entrance.

"HOW THE HELL do you know where I live, *and* the passcode to my gate?" Katarina asks from the back seat as Romeo continues down the driveway to her estate.

"Was it not common knowledge?" Romeo turns his head to look at her.

"No, it wasn't," she huffs.

"It took me five minutes. You should get a better system. Really, it's a surprise you've lasted as long as you have."

"It's never been an issue. They can't break in if they don't know where I live." She crosses her arms over her chest and glares out the window.

"It's more like entering when you have the access codes. There's no breaking involved," Romeo counters with a smirk, though I know he's being serious.

"Don't worry, bellezza. I'll upgrade your system for you. And not even this jackass will be able to crack it." I gesture to my brother.

"Challenge accepted." Romeo laughs.

Chapter Seven

Katarina

My thoughts are all over the place right now. I have no idea what's going on, what I'm thinking... Have I lost my mind? That has to be it. I've finally drunk the stardom Kool-Aid and completely lost it.

What other scenario would have me bringing two strangers—not just two strangers but two insanely hot, identical twin strangers—back to my house. Not that I think Romeo is hot, although he is the mirror image of Luca. There's just something different about him. My stomach doesn't twist and turn with nerves or excitement when I look at him. However, when I take those little stolen glances at Luca, it's like I've got a whole butterfly farm fluttering around, trapped inside me. I haven't figured out why he ignites these feelings, other than my earlier theory that I've gone insane. Which is a highly likely hypothesis at this point.

I make it exactly five steps into the foyer of the house before I hear them coming. My team. It's Amy I hear scream first. "You better hope to God you're not already dead, Katy, because I want the pleasure of killing you myself," she says as she rounds the corner and comes into view.

I don't miss how Luca steps closer, slightly in front of me. I'm not sure what form of danger he thinks the pixie-sized blur of color storming our way presents. Amy has a very unique sense of fashion. Basically, if she can get every color of the rainbow on her at once, then she's happy.

"Ah, not dead, Amy." I laugh.

"This isn't funny, Katy. Do you have any idea how worried I've been? How worried we've all been? You just disappeared. After that whole incident, you just vanished," she says, wiping a tear from her face.

I step around Luca, reaching Amy, and wrap my arms around her. "I'm sorry. I didn't have my phone. I didn't know what was going on. I'm sorry," I repeat.

Though, honestly, after I asked Romeo to make sure my team got out of the stadium safely, I haven't given them much thought. I've been so preoccupied with all that is Luca Valentino that I checked out of my own life. That's not like me. I've been so hyperfocused on being Kat Star for so long I haven't even taken a vacation in the last four years.

"Thank god you're alive. We need to get to work to address this. I've booked GMA for tomorrow morning. This afternoon, we've got three radio appearances. We need to issue a press release. I've written it up. You just have to sign off on it." Liam hands me a typed-out piece of paper.

"What?"

"Katy, you were shot at. Someone tried to assassinate you," he says matter-of-factly.

"I'm aware. I was there," I tell him.

"What the fuck is going on?" Luca growls from right behind me.

"Katy, why on earth are they here?" Liam asks.

"Who the fuck do you think you're talking to, asshole?" Luca steps in front of me again.

"Okay, stop. Liam, they're here to help. Amy, can you please show them to the mailroom. I'll deal with this later," I say, shoving the printed-out press release into Liam's chest. "I need a bath." I throw my hands up in the air as I walk away from everyone. I really do need some alone time. Some time to reevaluate what the hell is going on. Storming up the stairs and into my bedroom, I slam the door shut. "Thank you, Amy," I say aloud as I find my phone sitting on the charging dock on my bedside table.

Picking it up, I see a thousand missed calls and messages. All from random numbers, people who pretend they're my friends. When, in reality, I really only have a handful of people who actually care about me—well, two. Amy and Zane. There are a ton of calls from him too. Hitting his number, I return his call first. His voicemail connects.

"Zane, it's me. I'm sorry I didn't have a chance to check in earlier, but I'm fine. Totally, one hundred percent in one piece. No need for you to worry. Anyway, call me back when you can." I hang up and turn around. "What the..." I gasp, my hand flying to my mouth in shock when I find Luca standing in my room. Leaning his large—his very large—frame against the wall.

"Who's Zane?" he asks in a low, near monotone voice.

"A friend. Why?"

"What kind of friend?"

"The best kind of friend." I look at my bedroom door. It's shut.

How did I not hear him come in?

Luca tilts his head to the side and inspects me. "Is he your boyfriend?"

"What? God no." I laugh at the idea of anyone thinking Zane and I are anything more than friends.

"Do you have a boyfriend?" Luca presses further.

"Why?"

Lifting one shoulder into a half shrug, he smirks. "Just want to know if I need to make anyone conveniently disappear."

My eyes widen. "I can't even tell if you're joking or not."

"You didn't answer the question," he states.

"Do you have a girlfriend?"

"No," he says quickly. "See how easy it is to answer a question?"

"I know how to answer questions. I just like to make use of my free rights and all that."

"Cute." He smirks.

"Why are you in here, Luca?" I fold my arms over my chest.

"Because you are in here."

I shake my head. I don't have the energy for this. I really just need a bath. Spinning around, I walk into the bathroom and turn the faucet to the hottest setting. I then pour a generous portion of lavender bubble bath into the tub.

I can't believe this is happening to me. As I stand here and watch the tub fill with bubbles and steaming water, my mind conjures up memories I prefer not to think about. Memories I've done my best to bury in the deep recesses of my mind. It never works. Every time I see a bathtub, I see her. I see the blood, her lifeless body... But what I see most is her leaving me behind. Her weakness.

Shaking the thoughts from my head, I scan the

room. This isn't the shitty little bathroom in the tiny apartment we occupied when my mom was alive. No, this is luxury at its finest. This bathroom, full of white and grey marble, is larger than the whole trailer I shared with my father. I take a deep breath. The air doesn't smell of booze and cigarettes. It's clean.

I pull my shirt over my head. And just as I'm undoing the button on my jeans, I realize I'm not alone. Pivoting on my heel, I find Luca standing in the doorway. "I've met your mother and there is no way she hasn't taught you about privacy and respecting women," I say.

"Your point?"

"I'm trying to take a bath here, Luca. Get out!" I practically yell, exasperated by his antics at this point.

"Okay, I'll turn around. Let me know when you're covered by all those bubbles." He turns his back to me.

"Oh my god," I whisper under my breath. I'm not sure I've met anyone as… I don't have a word for what Luca is. He's just… too much.

I pull my jeans down, unhook my bra, and slide my underwear down my legs. Stepping into the bath, I sink under the water until it reaches above my head and burns my eyes. I like being fully submerged. Everything gets blocked out and I can just be.

When I come back up, I find Luca staring at the tub. "I never said you could turn around," I tell him, blinking the water out of my face.

"I'm going to wait out here. Don't drown," he grunts and walks away.

Picking up the remote next to the tub, I press play and let the music drown out the rest of my thoughts.

Chapter Eight

Luca

I lie back on Katarina's bed and observe her room. This is her inner sanctuary, and isn't what I expected to see of a pop star's bedroom. It's all pale pinks and whites. Everywhere. Right down to the sheer white curtains billowing in the open window.

It's surprisingly peaceful in here, surrounded by her things. There's a dressing table with small ornaments on it. Everything looks as though it's been perfectly positioned by an interior designer and hasn't been touched since. This could be a bedroom out of a magazine. There're no personal items, other than her phone sitting on the bedside table. I refrain from picking it up and going through her messages. She never answered my question about having a boyfriend or not.

And then there's her so-called friend. Zane. *Who the fuck is he?* I know I could have the answers within hours. All I'd have to do is make a call to one of our men, and they'd find out everything there is to know about Kat Star. I don't know if I want to do that, though. For the first time ever, I want to get to know a woman. I want to get to know her myself, not from a piece of paper that outlines her whole life up to the present moment.

Besides, I'm sure I could open any tabloid and read a lot about Katarina if I wanted to. Not that I'd ever believe what I read in that trash disguised as news. I might not be Kat Star level famous, but I've had my fair share of media attention. Being the son of Theo Valentino, the ruthless businessman and suspected mafia boss, comes with its downfalls. One of them being the paparazzi just waiting to catch you doing something—anything—that proves the rumors are true.

I close my eyes, exhaustion from the events of the past twenty-four hours catching up with me. Not to mention, the fucking hole I have in my body. I just need five minutes. Reaching into the back of my jeans, I draw the 9mm I took off my brother when we arrived, lift my head, and slip the gun under the pillow. I'll get a backup when Katarina finishes in the bathroom.

THAT SENSE of being watched falls over me. My eyes snap open and my hand reaches for the gun under my pillow. Only to retract it when I'm met with a pair of bright-green irises and the face of a fucking angel. Katarina is lying next to me, looking right at me. We continue to stare into each other's eyes, neither one of us blinking or turning away.

"Do you have a habit of watching people sleep?" I ask her, breaking the silence.

"Do you have a habit of sleeping in other people's beds?" she counters with a raised brow.

"Can't say I've ever slept in a woman's bed before, no." I smirk. Katarina rolls her eyes and her lips fight the smile she doesn't want to give me. "What time is it?" I ask.

"It's seven p.m."

"Fuck," I grunt, pushing myself upright. "Why didn't you wake me? I've been asleep all day?"

"You needed to sleep. You were shot yesterday, in case you've forgotten," she says, climbing off the bed.

I follow her, gripping the side of my waist. I probably should have moved slower. That shit fucking hurts. "Yeah, not so easy to forget, bellezza," I tell her.

"You should take something. I would offer you something but I don't keep any pain killers in this house." Her statement throws me off.

Why does she avoid pain killers? Is she an addict?

My eyes drift down the length of her bare arms. That's when I see it. A long scar that runs up the inside of her left wrist. Not an addict. A suicide attempt that wasn't successful, thank fucking god. Katarina notices where my eyes have landed and spins around. I follow her as she walks through a door. A closet. Not just any closet, a pop star's closet. She pulls a cardigan from a shelf and puts it on.

"You don't need to do that, you know," I tell her.

"Do what?" Her neck cranes to the side as she glares at me over her shoulder.

"Hide. You don't have to hide from me."

Her eyes widen briefly before she turns her head away from me again. "I'm not hiding. I don't have anything to hide. This is my bedroom, remember? What the hell would I even be hiding? Seriously, is there a reason you're in here?" Her voice gets louder with each word as she walks away, throwing her arms in the air before finally pivoting to face me again.

Standing there, with one hand cocked on her hip, her brows raised in question, her lips pursed. That long dark hair cascading over one shoulder. I can't help but smile as I watch her. She's fucking flawless. Even when she's trying to appear pissed off, she's the most beautiful thing I've ever seen.

"What on earth are you smiling about?" she asks.

"Just thinking about how fucking beautiful you are." I lift one shoulder.

Katarina rolls her eyes. "Your brother is downstairs. He wouldn't leave without you."

Does she really think she's getting rid of me? Yeah, that's not fucking happening.

"Have you eaten?" I ask her.

"Come on, I'll take you to Romeo." Katarina brushes past me.

Reaching out, I grab hold of her arm, halting her movements. "Wait." I have no idea what I'm doing. I should just follow her out of this room, away from that bed that I want to throw her down on and worship every inch of her body. I should do that, because it's the right thing to do.

However, what I actually do is the total opposite. I pull her against me, ignoring the pain that radiates through my rib cage with the movement. Katarina's mouth opens in shock, a small gasp parting her plump lips. I don't wait for the shock to wear off. Leaning down, I slam my mouth on hers, take a few steps, and push her against the wall. Closing her in as my tongue entwines with hers. Her small hands fist my shirt, pulling, pushing, then pulling again. She's warring with herself. Thank fuck the side of her that wants me to kiss her, that wants me to own her, is winning. My fingers dig into her hips. I'd give anything to pick her up, have her legs wrap around my waist. I can't do that right now. It would hurt but *I could.* However, I don't think she's ready for that yet.

So I also *can't…*

Pulling away, I linger near her mouth. I want more. So much fucking more. "It's not enough," I whisper.

Katarina opens her eyes. "Not even close," she says with a deep inhale. Her fingers open and close around the fabric of my shirt before she releases it.

Reaching up, I tuck her hair behind her ear. "Bellezza. Fucking pure beauty."

Katarina shakes her head. "If you really knew me, the real me, you wouldn't see beauty. The insides do not match the package," she says before wriggling her way out of my hold and walking out the door.

"Wait." I catch up to her but she doesn't turn around or slow down. "You know I was shot yesterday. I probably shouldn't be walking this fast."

That has her steps faltering. "Emotional manipulation, Luca, not cool."

"Emotional manipulation only works on people who care. Are you saying you care about me, Katarina?" I smirk, acting like the playboy jock I've been playing since I discovered girls at a very young age.

"I'm sure that smirk melts plenty of panties, Luca, but it won't work on me. Wanna know why?"

"Why?" I ask, truly intrigued. My smirk always fucking works.

"Because I'm not wearing any panties." She laughs and then walks off, leaving me staring after her.

My eyes go straight to her ass, currently wrapped

in a pair of yoga pants. Whoever the fuck designed these pants is a genius. Every curve, every toned inch of her ass and legs, perfectly displayed for my viewing pleasure.

"Fuck, bellezza, are you trying to torture me?" I readjust my growing cock before catching up to her again. I follow her down a long set of stairs. By the time we get to the bottom, I'm absolutely fucked. This whole getting shot thing is not for me. Let's hope it doesn't happen again. Although, I'd do it ten times over if it meant saving the woman in front of me.

Her soft laughter echoes off the walls of the hall. I didn't get much of a chance to look around this house this morning. It's lush like you'd expect someone of Katarina's fame to have, yet there's a subtleness to the décor that doesn't scream pop star or new money. I have so many questions in my head that I want to ask her. I want to know who her parents are, what her childhood was like. When she tried to kill herself, and if she still suffers from those thoughts. That last one's at the top of my fucking list.

"How many people live in this house?" I ask her.

"Just me. Why?"

"Anyone ever tell you it's fucking big. What the hell do you need all this space for anyway?" I complain, my chest heaving and aching at the same time.

"I don't need all this space. I want it. There's a difference," she says matter-of-factly.

"Well, I stand corrected. Why do you *want* all this space?" I press her.

"When you grow up without space, you tend to overcompensate when you're older. If you can, and I can. So I do." She shrugs. She doesn't realize that little tidbit tells me everything I need to know about her childhood. All these little pieces she's giving me will stay locked in my head. I will find the answers I want, and if I knew her longer than twenty-four hours, I'd be asking those questions.

The problem I have with that is I don't want to scare her off. I want to keep her around, which means I can't go into this all *guns blazing*. Speaking of, I was so fucking distracted by her in the bedroom that I left mine under her pillow. I look back down the hall and up the stairs. There is no way I'm making that trek again, unless I'm following Katarina, of course.

Chapter Nine

Katarina

I *kissed him.*

I just had his tongue in my mouth and he was the one who pulled away first. That's the thought that's on a constant loop in my mind. The feel of his hard body pressed up against mine, his taste, his scent surrounding me. It's all too much, but I want more.

I can't recall a time I've ever felt like this. I've

never wanted anyone the way I do Luca, and it's scaring the shit out of me.

Why do I want him?

I don't know him enough to want him. Logically, I'm aware of that blaring fact. Logic doesn't seem to have anything to do with the way my body is craving his touch. I'm not used to this. I have no idea what to do in this situation. Don't get me wrong, I've dated. A lot. I've dated frogs, toads, and a handful of nice guys. I've just never wanted them. I didn't care if they came or went. With Luca, I'm trying really hard not to come across as a stage-five clinger, when all I really want to do is *cling*.

This is foreign. I don't know whether to embrace these new feelings or run away as fast as I can. I think Luca Valentino will have the power to destroy me, if I let him in, worse than anyone ever has before. And that's saying a lot, because my father almost succeeded—if he hadn't died when I was sixteen, I wonder if he would have eventually. It's something I think about a lot.

Would I still be who I am today if my father hadn't driven into that tree that night? Probably not. I know one thing for certain. I wouldn't be here at all if it weren't for Zane.

Which brings me to my next point. It's really odd that he hasn't returned my call yet. Maybe I should reach out to Marcia and check that everything's okay. I know with Zane's position in the club, he's not only running a lot of stuff, but he's also a target for his rivals. He patched in not long after my dad died. He said it was something he always wanted to do. Though I think he did it to earn money. Money he used to take care of me. I've offered to pay him back, give him a way out of the lifestyle he leads. He turned me down and said if I ever offered him a cent again, we'd have serious issues. I haven't approached the subject since.

I lead Luca into the living room, where I left Romeo hours ago. He's still here, except he's not alone. There are four other men sharing the space. Scary-looking men, in black suits.

"Luc, man, heard you took some more lead," one of them says as we enter.

I have no idea what Luca says in response, because whatever it is, it's not in English. Romeo joins in, and I'm forced to wonder what everyone is saying. Considering there are six men in my living room, in a heated conversation, using a language I don't under-stand. I look from Luca to each of the other men. He seems to be getting really worked up. I don't know what to do here. For all I know, they could be discussing the weather. Highly doubtful, but possible, right?

Yeah, probably not. All the shouting brings back memories I try really fucking hard to suppress. I turn around and walk out of the living room. My living room. Whatever their issue is, they can work it out themselves. Heading into the kitchen, I find freshly squeezed orange juice in the fridge, pour myself a glass, and lean against the counter as I take small sips in an attempt to block out all the noise.

Amy sidles up a few moments later, positioning herself beside me with her eyes glued to the entrance of the room. "How are you doing with all of this?" She waves a hand in the general direction of where the living room would be through the walls.

"I don't know." I shrug.

"You have six insanely hot men arguing about God knows what, in Italian, in your living room right now," she whispers, like this is a fact I wasn't aware of.

"So I heard," I say.

"Want me to get rid of them? 'Cause I will. I'll kick them all out on their asses."

"I don't know," I tell her. I honestly don't know what I'm supposed to do here. "What time is GMA in the morning?" I ask her, changing the subject.

"We need to be in the studio by six."

"Great, just what I want to be doing right now," I groan.

"It's better to get on top of the story than have to dig your way out of it. There are already at least fifty different conspiracy theories making the headlines. Not to mention, the men you're currently housing in your private residence," she reminds me.

"What do you mean?" I ask. I've purposely been avoiding social media, news channels, everything really.

"There are rumors that he's connected to the

mafia." She lowers her voice and her eyes dart from side to side.

At this, I laugh. That's ridiculous. He's a football player, not a mobster. My laughter dies in my throat at the solemnness of Amy's expression. "Seriously?" I whisper.

She nods her head. "It's what they're saying, and not just connected, but really well connected. They say his father's one of the five bosses of the under-world in New York."

"That can't be true." Even as I say the words, I recall all the conversations, the things that made me question what everyone was talking about. The men who always seem to be around him, dressed in suits, with stern faces. His aunt's comments about "catching bullets' and the fact that, besides his mother, none of his family seems that concerned about him being shot. They all acted like it happens on a regular basis, like a scraped knee or a broken bone. As I'm mulling this over, the man in question walks into the kitchen, his eyes immediately locking on mine. "Are you in the mafia?" I blurt out without thinking.

Luca's steps halt. His gaze roams from mine to Amy's and back again. He's inspecting every feature of my face without saying a word.

"Ah, I'm going to get your wardrobe ready for tomorrow and set your alarm." Amy disappears quicker than I've ever seen her move.

"What would give you the impression that I'm in the mafia?" Luca finally asks.

"A lot, actually," I say.

We stare at each other, neither of us moving. "Such as?" He pushes me for more.

"There's the fact that no one really seems too concerned that you were shot, Luca, and everyone keeps mentioning this wasn't the first time. There's the scary men in suits who seem to pop up wherever you are. The fact that you and your brother think you can do a better job at figuring out which one of my crazy stalker fans wants to kill me." I bring the cup to my lips and finish the last of my juice.

"Well, when you list it out like that, it does sound like something out of a bad mafia movie." Luca strolls over to the fridge and opens it. "I'm making you dinner," he announces.

"What?" I don't know if it's me, if I'm losing my mind, or if he's actually this insane.

"I'm making you dinner, spaghetti. It's basically the only thing I know how to cook. My nonna taught me." His head pops around the fridge and he gives me that smirk of his again.

"I can't eat pasta," I tell him.

"Why? Are you allergic? Wait… Are you allergic to anything?" His eyebrows draw down like he's seriously considering the possibility.

"No, it's just not on the approved food list." I shrug.

"What's the *approved food* list? And why the fuck do you need a list of approved foods?" He shuts the fridge.

"The nutritionist gives me a list. I need to stay in shape, so I eat what's on the list."

"That's the stupidest thing I've ever heard. There's nothing wrong with your shape—trust me, it's fucking perfection, bellezza. A little bit of pasta isn't going to change that."

"It's fine. You don't have to cook for me. Also, you haven't answered my question."

Luca steps into my space. I inhale, which is a mistake. Because all I get is a whiff of him, his scent that I can't seem to get enough of. "I'll answer your question. But if we're doing a little Q&A, I'm going to have a few questions of my own." He grips my arm, my left arm. Holding my hand, he shifts the fabric of my sweater and lightly runs his fingertips over the jagged scar on my wrist. "What happened here?" he asks quietly.

"Isn't it obvious?" I fire back, attempting to pull away from his touch.

Luca tightens his grasp. "I want to hear it from you," he says before bringing my wrist up to his lips, where he kisses along the rough edges of scar tissue. His tenderness brings tears to my eyes. No one has ever tried to kiss away the pain that scar brings me. The memory of my weakest time. A reminder of how close I came to ending up just like her, my mother.

"I tried to kill myself when I was fourteen." My voice cracks. I don't think I've ever talked about this to anyone other than Zane.

"Thank you," Luca says, dropping my arm to my

side as he intertwines our fingers. He lowers his face to mine and my tongue delves out, wetting my lips. All I can focus on right now is that mouth of his. He stops just millimeters from making contact. "Are you a good actor, Katarina? I know you can sing, and I know you can dance, but can you act?" he asks.

"I don't know. Why?"

"Because if I answer your question truthfully, you're going to have to act like you don't know. You're going to have to act like everything is normal and you're oblivious. Otherwise, we're both going to be in a lot of shit." His words are whispered. If he weren't so close, I wouldn't have heard them at all.

I think about what he said. Am I a good actor? If I had to, I could lie like no other. To protect him. The guy did take a bullet for me. It's only fair to do the same. The thing is... I don't even care what his answer is right now. I mean, I know what it is. It couldn't be any more obvious. I just don't need to hear him say the words. I don't need him to confirm it. What I need is for him to kiss me again. So, instead of answering him, I push up on my tiptoes, wrap my arms around his neck, and close the small gap that was separating our lips.

Chapter Ten

Luca

I'm really fucking glad Katarina kissed me, because I would have told her the truth. Which is fucking dangerous for both of us. For my family. I've never wanted to tell anyone before. I know people have their suspicions, which I never confirm nor deny. But when Katarina just flat-out asked, all I wanted to do was say yes and hope to God it didn't scare her away.

Instead of making me tell her, she's kissing me.

My arms wrap around her waist. Picking her up, I set her on the counter behind us. My hands tangle in her hair, tilting her head in just the right position to grant me better access to her mouth. My tongue duels with hers, and the sweet taste of oranges assaults my tongue. I don't want to part from her. I want to stay fused together like this forever.

A throat clears behind me. Pulling away from Katarina, I look up to see Romeo standing there with his hands in his pockets and his brows raised in question. With a groan, I place Katarina's feet back on the floor. I try to hold back the grunt of pain. I don't succeed.

"You shouldn't be lifting heavy things. You just had surgery," Katarina scolds.

I take my time, letting my eyes roam over her body. "You're hardly a heavy thing, bellezza." Then I pivot to face Romeo. "You heading out?" I ask him, already knowing what he wants to say but won't with an audience.

"Yeah, I need to swing by and see Pops first. You coming?" he asks.

I look back at Katarina. I don't want to leave her. I really fucking don't. "Nah, I'll catch up with you later," I say, my eyes returning to my brother. With a nod of his head, he pivots and walks out.

"You don't need to stay here, you know. I have a lot to do actually. You should go with him," Katarina says.

"I told you I'm cooking you dinner. Where is this

list of approved foods of yours?" I ask her. It's the most ridiculous thing I've ever fucking heard. I'm an athlete. I know all about taking care of your body and shit, but approved foods? That's bullshit, and I'll be putting a stop to it as soon as I can.

Pasta... I mean, who the fuck doesn't eat fucking pasta?

My nonna would have a damn near coronary if she heard that. Her pasta sauce is a family staple. Everyone fights for those leftovers. Matteo once pulled a gun out on all of us to make sure he got the last bit to take home. After that incident, Nonna has made sure there are five containers, one for each of us boys and our cousin Izzy.

"Ah, I'm really not all that hungry, honestly. I'll just grab a fruit bowl. But you should eat. Help yourself to whatever you want. Or order in. Are your friends gone?" Katarina asks.

"They're putting in your new security system," I tell her.

"My new security system? Which is what exactly?"

"Apart from me? A state-of-the-art device that not even Romeo will be able to hack into."

"And how to you play into this new... system?" she asks with a skeptical brow.

"Trust me, babe, no one is gonna get past me to get to you."

"You know you can't just follow me everywhere, right? Even if I wanted you to, which I'm not saying I do, I have a really busy schedule and you can't always be there."

"You're right. I can't always be there. And when I'm not, I'll have two of the guys with you instead."

"That's not necessary."

"From what I've just seen come out of that mail room of yours, I think a whole fucking army is necessary." I wish I could fucking unsee all the disturbing shit Romeo showed me, and I've seen a lot of disturbing shit in my twenty-odd years on this earth.

"It's mostly just over-the-top fans." Katarina shrugs, as if it's no big deal.

"Someone tried to shoot you yesterday. *Yesterday.* I don't think you understand the seriousness of the situation."

"I know. What do you want me to do? Break down and refuse to come out of my room? Hide away and let them win? I won't do that. I've worked too freaking hard to get to where I am, and I'm not stopping because some jerk has a hard-on for killing me," she yells.

"That's not... I'm not telling you to stop being you. I'm just saying I'd like you to give me a little time. Give *us* a little time to find this fucker."

"You wanna play hero, Luca, go for it. But I'm not asking you to. I'm not looking for some white knight to come in and save the day."

I can't help but smile. "I'm no white knight, babe. The thoughts I have about you are anything but chivalrous."

I watch as the blush colors her neck, making its way up to her face. "I have an early start and a lot to do so… you really can go home. You don't have to stay here." She turns to grab a precut fruit bowl from the fridge. When she shuts the door, she turns on her heels and heads in the opposite direction.

"Do you want me to leave?" I ask her. I don't want to leave, but I will if it's what she wants. Maybe.

"I… I don't know," she says and walks away.

Fuck me.

I'm about to follow her when my phone blares in my pocket. Groaning, I hit the green answer button. "Coach, how're things?" I know I'm in deep shit for not checking in with the team yet.

"*How're things?* Valentino, you have a lot of fucking explaining to do. What on this God-given earth made you think it'd be a good idea to jump in front of a bullet right before a game?"

"Ah, the fact that a woman's life was at stake, Coach," I grunt. I will not apologize for saving her. Ever.

"Right, fuck, Valentino, this is going to set you back. What are the doctors saying? I couldn't get shit out of them. Which in itself is fucked up. The team always has access to medical files—everyone signs a release as part of their contract. Care to explain why you're so special the hospital won't share yours?"

"I don't know what you want me to say, Coach."

"Tell me what the docs are telling you? How long will you be out? 'Cause I gotta be honest here,

Valentino. You haven't played one game and you're already benched. It's not looking good."

I knew this was coming. I'm not a fucking idiot. No team is going to keep on a liability. They're paying me good fucking money to play football. If I can't play, then it's smart for them to try to cut their losses now. My contract is for this season only, so I have until the end of it to get back out on that field or give up my career forever. I won't get another shot at this.

Running a hand through my hair, I pull at the strands. "I'll be back on that field next week."

"That's highly unlikely. You're going to need a med clearance. You were fucking shot, Valentino. We're not talking about a sprained ankle here."

"I'm aware. Look, I'll be fine. I'll be there," I say again. "I'll get the clearance. Don't worry about it."

"I'm sending you to the team's doctor. He's the only one who can clear you. I'll email you the appointment time. Don't miss it."

"I won't."

"And, Valentino, if you're not holed up in a hospital bed, I expect to see you sitting on the side-lines. You know the drill. This isn't a vacation." He disconnects the call.

Fuck, I'm going to have to be on the field at five in the morning. I glance at my watch. It's eight p.m. now. I need to find Katarina. Maybe I can convince her to come to the stadium with me. As I think on that, I pull my phone out and text Romeo.

ME:

I have to be at the stadium for practice at five tomorrow.

His response comes in immediately.

RV:

Last I checked, I wasn't your secretary or keeper.

ME:

Don't be an ass. I need one of you to come hang out with Katarina.

RV:

I'll sort it out.

That's what I love about my family. Ask and you shall receive. I know that one of my brothers will be here before I have to head out in the morning. I told Katarina I'd leave her with a few of my men, and I will. I just want the assurance of having one of my brothers here too, especially if I can't be here myself.

I have no idea where she's gone. I'm aimlessly walking down halls, peeking into rooms, when I run into... Actually, I don't know who this chick is.

"She's in the studio," Rainbow Brite answers my unspoken question, her arms piled high with clothes.

"Which is where exactly?" I ask her.

"Take a left down there." She tips her head in the direction I was going. "Second door on the right."

"Thank you." I nod, motion to take another step,

and pause. "Wait... What is it that you do for Katarina?"

"I'm her personal assistant. Why?" She seems to straighten her spine when she speaks.

"No reason. The other douche who was here earlier, what's he do?"

"Liam? That's her manager." The woman smiles. "And, yes, he can be a bit of a douche, but he's good and has Katy's best interests at heart."

"Okay, thanks."

"Oh, I almost forgot! Housekeeping gave me this." Shuffling the pile of clothing she's holding into one hand, Katarina's assistant removes a Ziplock from her bag and lifts it to eye level—my gun is closed inside. I raise my brows in question. "They found it on Katy's bed. Do me a favor and don't leave *this* lying around."

I pull the gun out and hand the plastic bag back to her. "Thanks," I say, tucking the weapon into the back of my jeans.

Opening the door to the studio, I'm even more thankful to be presently armed. I don't think I've ever drawn my gun so quick in my life.

"Two seconds is how long it will take me to pull this trigger and blow your fucking head off," I growl at the fucker who's got his arms around my girl.

Katarina. My girl. Yeah, I fucking like the idea of her being mine.

Chapter Eleven

Katarina

I freeze at Luca's growled threat. *Shit. This isn't happening.* I don't have time to react before Zane is shoving me behind him and drawing his own gun.

"Stop, no!" I scream, scrambling around Zane. I shock myself when I place my body in front of Luca.

"Bellezza, move," he grunts.

I'm telling myself it's because I know Zane won't shoot me. That's why I'm doing this. I also know Zane won't think twice before shooting Luca. I'm not sure who would have the quicker trigger finger, but something tells me it would be a close call.

"Wait, Zane, put it down. Now!" I yell.

"Zane? This is Zane? Your so-called best friend?" Luca's arm wraps around my waist and he picks me up, maneuvering his body in front of mine and holding me in place, so I can't get around him again.

"Sugarpops, care to explain why the fuck you have a Valentino in your house?" Zane asks.

Luca responds before I can form a coherent answer. "You know who I am. Good, then you know I'm not fucking around when I tell you that I'll take great pleasure in filling your body with holes."

"I'm sure you would," Zane says. "Let her go." His voice deepens to a more threatening tone and his jaw muscles tighten with the command.

Luca just laughs. I swear the guy has a death wish or something. I manage to worm my way out of his hold. I don't bother standing in front of either of them this time. Instead, I position myself to the side as I point a finger from one to the other. "Just so you know. If either of you shoots the other, I will never forgive you. So you both need to give up this macho bullshit now, or get the hell out of my house."

Zane looks at me with wide eyes. I've never picked anyone over him before, not that I'm choosing Luca over him now, but to him that's what it must feel like.

"Got a problem with that?" I press him.

"Yeah, a big fucking problem. You know who he

is, right? Come on, Katy, you're smarter than this. You know better than to get involved with someone like him."

"He saved my life yesterday, Zane."

"So what? You repay him by letting him into your bed?" Zane scoffs, and I blink. I can't believe he just said that to me. Luca moves fast, lightning fast. He drops his gun to the floor, and his right fist comes up and connects with Zane's jaw. Zane's head snaps to the side with the blow. He's quick to recover, though, and he cranes his neck to glare at Luca. "Really, you wanna do this? Fine. Let's do it."

"She said I couldn't shoot you, not that I couldn't knock you the fuck out. Which I will happily do if you ever disrespect her like that again," Luca grunts, as he takes a step back and crosses his arms in challenge.

"Okay, I'm out of here. Zane, you know where the guest rooms are. Show yourself to one." I look at him pointedly. I'm not impressed with what he just said to me, and right now I don't have the energy to deal with him.

"I could show him the front door, bellezza," Luca offers.

"Nope, he's family. He's staying." I glance back to see Zane smirking at Luca, who glares at him in disgust. "I'm going to bed," I tell them both.

"I think that's your cue to leave," Zane says to Luca.

"Yeah, you'd like that, wouldn't you." Luca laughs and proceeds to follow me out.

Once we get to my bedroom, I walk into my closet and close the door. I need some freaking time to think. I should send Luca home. I know I'll be safe with Zane here. That's not really why I want Luca to stay though. I don't want him here because I'm scared. Which, honestly, I'm shitting myself at the thought of someone looking to kill me. I want him here because the thought of him leaving and me never seeing him again makes my stomach turn.

I throw on a black satin and lace nightie and exit the closet to find Luca stripped down to his jeans with the top button undone. I know he's not wearing boxers under those. I saw him get dressed earlier today. The right side of his body is covered in a bandage that's already soaked through and in desperate need of redressing.

"You need to change that," I say, a finger directed at his side.

"Got a first aid kit?" he asks as his eyes roam up and down the length of me, and suddenly I feel self-conscious.

"In the bathroom. Come on." I lead him towards the vanity, reaching for the robe that hangs on the back of the door, shoving my arms through the sleeves, and tugging it closed.

"Don't feel like you have to cover all of that on my account. I really don't mind." Luca smirks at me.

"I'm sure you don't," I say as I bend down and retrieve the first aid kit from under the cabinet. "I'm sure I have something in here." I unzip the kit and start unpacking the supplies.

"I can do this. You don't need to help me." Luca grips my hand when I reach up to peel the bandage from the front of his body.

"I don't mind."

He releases my wrist and I work in silence, neither of us saying anything as I clean his wound before applying fresh dressings. I pack everything away and wash my hands. As I'm drying them on a towel, Luca asks, "Care to tell me how you know how to do that so well?"

"Nope," I answer.

He squints his eyes at me, and I get the feeling *no* is not a word Luca Valentino has heard often enough in his life. "I have to go to practice in the morning," he says.

"You're hardly in a condition to be running around a field," I tell him.

"I have to sit on the sidelines. Not my choice." He shrugs.

"Okay." I'm not really sure what to say. Why is he telling me this?

"I'll have one of my brothers here before I head out. I want you to take them with you wherever it is you gotta go tomorrow."

"I don't need a babysitter, Luca. I'm also not your responsibility. I'm sure Liam will have increased security already booked."

"And how well did that security look out for you yesterday?"

"That was different."

"It doesn't matter. I can't go to practice if I'm worried that you're out in the world by yourself."

"I've been out in the world by myself for a really long time now, Luca. I think I'll manage." I brush past him and throw my robe to the ground in my bedroom.

"I don't doubt that you're capable of looking after yourself, bellezza. I just want you to let me help."

I watch as Luca climbs into my bed after me. Like this is a routine we've done a million times before. "This is weird. Right? I think I've lost my mind," I groan, then roll onto my back to stare at the ceiling.

"It's crazy. But a good crazy."

"We don't know each other. Why are you even still here? In my bed?"

"I... I can't bring myself to leave," he admits, then counters with, "Why haven't you thrown me out yet?"

"I don't think I want you to leave. Which is insane."

"I think I was destined to meet you, Katarina. I think you might just be my person," he says, pulling me onto my side so I'm facing him. His hand comes up as he runs his fingers through my hair.

"And what person is that?" I question him.

"The one I'm going to spend the rest of my life with."

"I think that people experience crazy emotions when facing a near-death situation. That's what this is. We're in shock or something. It's not healthy for me to be codependent on a guy I don't even know. On anyone really," I say on a sigh.

"A little bit of codependency is good for you. Well, it's good for *me*, so depend away, bellezza."

"Why do you call me that? Bellezza?"

"Because you are the beauty to my beast."

"You're hardly a beast, Luca." I laugh at his ridiculousness.

"You're only looking surface deep. It's what's underneath, what's in my soul, that's ugly."

"Mmm, I think your soul is fine. You're a good person."

"You might be the only one to think that. Other than my family. But they have to love me," he says with a grin.

"That's not true. Not all families love like yours. Not all parents protect their children."

"No, but they should. It's what family is supposed to do."

"I've never had that. The only person whose ever loved me like that is Zane."

I feel Luca's body tense at the mention of my best friend. "Are you in love with him? Zane?" he asks point-blank.

"No." I laugh. "He's happily married, with a son and another baby on the way."

"Have you ever been?"

"No. He's always been like a big brother to me. That guy's saved me more times than I can count. Seen me at my worst and still stuck around. I wouldn't be who I am today without him," I admit, hoping Luca understands my relationship with Zane.

"I don't like him. Not to mention, his job is dangerous, Katarina. He's the president of an MC."

"Really? Because I got the impression that you two were thrilled to meet each other. I really sensed a great bromance forming there," I sass.

"Huh, you may wanna stick to singing. Being a comedian isn't in your future," Luca deadpans.

"Shit, I'll have to tell Liam to cancel that movie deal he just landed me. It's a romcom. I really thought I could do it. But if you insist I'm not funny enough, I'll pull out," I tell him, chewing on my bottom lip.

"What? No, you can fucking do anything you put your mind to. I'm sure of it. Don't give up on anything because of me," he stresses.

I laugh. "Guess that answers your earlier question."

"What question?" His eyebrows draw down in confusion.

"If I could act."

Luca blinks his eyes exactly three times before his hands are on my waist and he rolls his weight on top of me, his hips settling between my legs. Which seem to have a mind of their own as they spread open and invite him in.

Chapter Twelve

Luca

My body rests on top of hers, and my lips find her mouth as my hands grip her hips. Shifting my weight, I roll to my back, pulling her with me. She's now straddling me. Giving me unrestricted access. My hands slide up and down her sides, moving around to her back, where I squeeze the round globes of her ass and tug her into me. Grinding her center against the hardness of my cock.

"Fuck, I want you," I murmur between heated kisses.

Her fingers are careful as they explore my bare chest, avoiding my wound. "I don't want to hurt you," she whispers, pulling away from my mouth. She straightens her back to sit upright.

The view I have right now is fucking amazing. "You're not going to hurt me," I tell her, as my hands reach up to slide the thin straps of her little black scrap of lace she's wearing down her arms, exposing her naked breasts. I cup each in my hands. "Fuck me. Fucking perfection."

I feel the weight of her breasts in my palms while massaging the hard peaks of her nipples. They're not large, hard, fake tits like many other girls in her life-style have. They're real, soft yet firm, and fucking perky. A perfect C-cup. Enough to fill my hands. Enough to push together when I'm sliding my cock through them. I moan at the thought.

"Guess you're a boob man then, huh?" Katarina asks.

"I'm a Katarina man. You are fucking mine. Made for me. I couldn't have customized a more perfect body than this," I tell her, moving my hands along her flat stomach and down the insides of her thighs.

"Mmm, you're not so bad yourself," she says.

My hands travel back up, creeping underneath the soft fabric of her nightgown. I move slow, giving her plenty of time to stop my progression if she wants to.

She doesn't. My fingers find their way to the apex of her thigh, moving across to her bare pussy. Her bare, smooth pussy. I slide two digits through her wet folds and close my eyes.

"You're drenched, bellezza," I groan.

"Sorry?" She says it like she's not sure if it's a good thing or a bad thing.

"Don't be. I fucking love it. I need it. Climb on my face. I need to taste you," I tell her, lifting her hips and trying to guide her into position.

"What?"

"You heard me. Get up here and sit on my face. I'm fucking dying here, Katarina. I need to taste you. Now." This time, I don't give her the opportunity to think about my request. Using whatever strength I have, I pull her up to my face and place her down on my mouth. My tongue darts out and licks her opening and over her clit, circling around. "Fucking delicious," I growl into her pussy, going harder. Licking, sucking, nibbling at her. "I want you to come all over my face."

My eyes are locked on the image of her above me. She really does look like a fucking angel from this angle. So goddamn good.

"Oh god!" Her head tips back, her eyes closed and her mouth slightly open, as her whole body begins to tremble.

Pushing two fingers into her opening, I curl them up as my mouth sucks down on her clit. Within seconds, she's pushing her pussy into my face harder, her legs squeezing my head and locking it in place.

Not that I was going anywhere. This is the best fucking thing I've ever tasted.

"Luca, yes!" Katarina screams, and I have the urge to pound my fucking chest like a caveman. Hearing her call out my name in her moment of pleasure is everything I didn't know I was missing in my life. Once Katarina comes down from her high, she carefully slides off my body, doing her best to avoid my wound. "That was... so good." She smiles down at me.

"You're welcome." I smirk as my hands find their own way back to her breasts, massaging as soon as they make contact. Katarina reaches down, unzips my jeans, and slips a hand inside before wrapping it around my cock. "Fuck."

My hips thrust up at her touch, and the movement sends an immediate sharp pain along my side. I need to pay attention to what I'm doing. She must notice the pain on my face, because she freezes. "You need to stop moving. If you move, I'll stop. If you can stay still, I'll keep going," she says.

"I won't move," I tell her as quickly as I can. Fuck, I'd do anything to get her to glide that hand of hers up and down my cock.

"Good, make sure you don't because I really, really want to feel this..." She squeezes me tighter. "...inside me."

"Well, fuck me, bellezza. *Literally.* Sit that pretty little pussy of yours on my cock and ride me," I practically beg her.

"I know this sounds cliché. But just so you know, I don't usually do this," Katarina says, slowly pumping a hand over my cock.

"Do what?" I ask.

"Jump into bed with men so quickly. I'm not that girl."

I grab hold of her wrist, stopping her movements. "You know I don't expect this. We can stop. I don't want you to do anything you don't want to do."

"Besides singing, I've never wanted to do anything as badly as I want to do *you* right now, Luca."

Releasing her wrist, I place my hand back on her hip. "Far be it for me to deny a woman what she wants." I raise an eyebrow, almost daring her to take me.

Katarina guides the tip of my shaft to the entrance of her pussy before sinking down on me in an agonizingly slow pace. My fingers dig into her hips and I shove her all the way down, forcing her to fall forward as she bottoms out on me, her hands landing on my chest.

"Fuck yes," I groan.

Katarina's head lolls back as she moans, her nails embedding into my skin. "So good," she says as she slightly lifts her hips up my shaft before sliding down again and then repeating the process.

My fingers dig into the flesh of her hips. It's taking everything in me not to move, not to roll her over and fuck her hard and fast. Not that this, her moving up and down on my cock, isn't fucking good. It's almost too fucking good.

Reaching a hand between our bodies, I find her clit, rubbing slow, small circles. "I need you to come for me, bellezza," I tell her. I'm so close to exploding myself, but I need her to come again first. I will always make sure she comes first. No matter how fucking hard it is to restrain my urge to jump over that cliff.

"Shit, oh god. Fuck!" she screams, her pussy tightening around my cock and quivering as her orgasm rolls over her.

"Fuck!" I lift her off my cock just in time for the long ropes of cum to shoot out of me. Katarina falls beside me on the bed, her chest rising and falling with her heavy breaths.

"Are you okay? Did I hurt you?" Her head rolls to the side to look at me.

"More than okay," I tell her, reaching out to entwine my fingers with hers.

"Do you think we're crazy? It really is insane how much I think I like you."

"*Think* you like me…? Babe, wait until I'm back to one hundred percent and really show you what I'm made of. I guarantee you there will be no *thinking* involved." I wink.

Katarina laughs. It's a sound I want to record, just so I can play it over and over again. I know I can hop onto Spotify, listen to any of her songs, and hear her voice. But that's not what I want. I want this sound right here, the uncut version. The authentic happiness that's radiating off her.

"You've been shot before, right?" she asks me.

"Mmhmm."

"So, in your expert experience, how long does a full recovery take? Just out of curiosity…"

"Give me a week." I lean over and kiss the top of her head.

"BELLEZZA, I HAVE TO GO," I whisper, placing featherlight kisses on her forehead.

She squints her eyes open, staring at me for a minute, dazed. "Where are you going?"

"I gotta go to practice, babe. I'll find you as soon as I'm done."

"Oh, you don't have to do that. I have a huge day ahead of me. I have back-to-back appearances." She yawns.

"I'll find you anyway. My brother's downstairs. If you need anything, just yell."

"Which one?"

"Huh?"

"Which brother?" she asks.

"Theo."

"The scary one, great." She rolls over onto her back and glares at the ceiling.

"They're all scary. Some of them just hide it better." I smirk.

"You're not scary."

"*You* just don't have a reason to fear me, and you never will. I promise." I lean down and give her one more kiss. "I'll see you later." Then I force myself to walk away, my hand rubbing at my heart. There's a strange ache there. I don't fucking understand this need to be around her. I can go to practice. It's something I've been doing all my damn life.

Theo is waiting in the foyer for me when I reach the bottom of the stairs. "How you doing?" he asks.

"I've been better." I shrug.

"Are you taking anything for the pain?"

"I don't need pain pills. I'll be fine," I tell him. I'm not a fan of drugs of any kind. I've seen too many of my friends go down that road. It tends to happen when you're a bored, overprivileged teen with unlimited funds and no parental supervision.

"Suit yourself," Theo says, staring at me in that way he does when he's looking to unnerve someone. "What's the deal with her?" He nods towards the staircase.

"She's... different. I don't know. I can't explain it. Just make sure nothing happens to her. Please."

Theo's eyes widen. I've never asked anything like this before. I've never been interested in a girl for more than one night. I was wondering if these weird-ass feelings would be gone when I woke up, after having a taste of her the previous day. They didn't. If anything, I want her even more now than I did yesterday.

"I won't let anything happen to her. You have my word," Theo says. "She's family, and you know we protect family. Always."

"Thank you," I say. "I gotta go. Coach is already going to rip me a new asshole." I groan at the thought of having to face the guys. I've been ignoring my teammates' calls and messages since the incident.

Chapter Thirteen

Katarina

"I'm sorry. I am, but I really have to go and I can't exactly take you with me. You know that. It was your idea to keep our connection out of the public eye. How exactly is you following me around all day supposed to stick to that plan?" I ask Zane, who is currently pouting and fuming at the same time.

We've been arguing for fifteen minutes because Zane thinks he needs to be my new bodyguard. Not to mention, he is less than impressed by the brooding, almost-silent shadow Luca's delegated to me. The eldest Valentino brother has been like a statue in the corner of the room. Watching. Waiting. He reminds me of a cobra, just itching for its opportunity to strike. Even Zane is holding back in front of Theo. The two know each other. I haven't asked how, and frankly I don't think I want to know. But the way they greeted each other by name without needing a formal introduction tells me there's history there.

"But turning up with *him* is okay for your image?" Zane asks, pointing to the corner of the room. I look over to Theo. He's dressed impeccably in a well-fitted designer suit. Not a hair out of place. Does he look lethal? Yes. But he's also refined, and I guess he could come across as a businessman if you didn't know any better.

Turning back to Zane, I mouth, "I'm sorry." I don't know what else to say.

"That's enough. Katy, you have nothing to apologize for. Besides, Valentinos don't apologize. We're never wrong," Theo says, and as I turn my head back to look at him in confusion—because, let's face it, the man has hardly said anything for the fifteen minutes I've been downstairs—he's taking large steps to approach us. "I don't know what the fuck this is." Theo gestures between me and Zane. "But she's practically family. I'm sure I don't need to remind you what happens to people who think they can shit on my family, Zane." Theo tilts his head slightly.

"Yeah, well, she *is* my family, nothing practical about it. So you're intimidation won't work here, Valentino."

"Oh, I'm not looking to intimidate anyone. I'm just reminding you who you're talking to. We might be under a mutual agreement at the moment, but that can change with the snap of my fingers." Theo demonstrates the gesture. "Just like that, everything you've worked for... *gone*."

"Yeah, still don't give a fuck. Threaten me all you want," Zane grunts. "Kat, someone tried to fucking shoot you. You shouldn't even be leaving this house. Fuck, you should come home. At least until we find out who the fuck is trying to kill you."

"You know I can't go back there, Zane. I can't." I shake my head. I haven't returned to my hometown since Zane put me on a bus, with a bunch of cash and a key to an apartment here in New York, nearly four years ago. I really do owe him everything, and I feel like shit arguing with him right now. I don't like it. "We'll talk. I promise. But I do need to go."

"You don't need him, Kat. You don't need any of them. If you're scared, I can get you out of here. Just say the word."

"If I'm scared? Of course I'm fucking scared, Zane. I'm terrified of losing everything I've worked so damn hard to obtain. Of losing everything *you've* sacrificed to give me this life. I can't go back. I can't."

Zane wraps his arms around me. "I'm sorry. I

didn't mean to upset you. I just… I don't like feeling so fucking helpless."

"You showing up helps more than anything," I tell him. It's not like I have a line of people willing to take a bullet for me. Though, with the Valentinos, I just might.

"Katy, we need to go now." Liam's voice cuts in.

"Okay, I'm coming." I untangle myself from Zane. "You should go home. Marcia needs you more than I do right now, and if you miss seeing that baby falling out of her because of me, I'll never forgive myself." I smile. His wife is due to give birth any minute. The fact he even left her to come to me tells me how worried he is.

"I can't just leave you here alone."

"I'm not alone," I tell him. I shouldn't be leaning on Luca so much. For all I know, he got what he wanted out of me last night and I'm never going to see him again. But if that were the case, I'm not so sure his brother would be here right now.

"Yeah, I see that." Zane runs a hand through his hair. He's torturing himself over the decision to stay or leave.

"Look, you came. You've seen for yourself that I'm still very much in one piece. No one else would have done that for me. Only you. So thank you for that. But, honestly, I'm fine, and you have a family to get back to."

"You are my family," he reminds me.

"I know that. Please, just go back to Marcia and

we'll talk. I'll call you, and once that baby is born, we'll find somewhere to catch up." I smile. I'm supposed to be on tour in six weeks. I'm not sure how I'll swing a vacation, even for a weekend, but I don't tell him that now.

"Okay. But if you need anything, you call me," he says. It's not a question.

"You know I will," I tell him because if I were really in need, I would.

SITTING on the sofa in the studio of Good Morning America is not where I want to be right now.

Where do I want to be?

Back in bed with Luca would be a good option. I'm finding it hard to concentrate. I'm bluffing my way through this interview.

"What are your thoughts on the man who saved you? Luca Valentino? Do you know him personally? Why would a random football player risk his life like that? It plays into the rumors that the Valentino family is into some shady business dealings, with ties to the Italian mafia," Juliet, the female host, asks me.

"Well, that's a lot of questions to unpack there, Juliet. What do I think of Luca Valentino?" I pause, pretending I actually need a moment to think about it. "I think he's courageous, a hero—well, my hero anyway. I'm thankful to him for doing what he did. If he hadn't been so brave, chances are I wouldn't be sitting here right now." I offer the audience my well-practiced smile.

"You say courageous; some say reckless. What do you know about his injuries? Have you visited him in the hospital?"

"I did, and he seems to be in good spirits. From what I hear, he'll make a full recovery."

"Well, I know I speak for women all over the world when I say I wouldn't mind being saved by a man who looks like that," Juliet says, glancing wistfully at the full-size image of Luca in his uniform currently plastered on the screen beside us.

"I'm not sure what the question is there." All attempts to keep the annoyance out of my tone are in vain. I can see it on the hosts' faces; they pick up on it too.

"Are you involved with Mr. Valentino?" the cohost, George, asks me.

"Involved? What do you mean?" I play dumb.

"Are you romantically involved with Mr. Valentino?" he attempts to clarify.

"Until yesterday, I'd never met the man, and he's currently recovering from a bullet wound. How do you imagine I became romantically involved with someone who's just been shot? And in such a short amount of time?" I manage to deflect the question, turning their stupidity back on them.

"Right, of course. Well, we thank you for coming in today and sharing your story. It must have taken a lot of courage to be out in public after the incident," George says, putting an end to the interview.

"Thank you, it's been a pleasure to be here." I'm not sure how else to reply to that comment, so I leave it at that.

The moment the director calls cut, I walk off the stage in a huff. I hate these things. I hate interviews. And I hate how they try to put words in my mouth or trip me up. I've never had to be more on my game than during meetings with the press.

The moment I enter the dressing room, Hailey hands me a bottle of water. "Thank you." I offer her a polite smile. She's the only one who hasn't asked me how I am or wanted to discuss what's now being referred to as *the incident*.

I go and sit on the sofa, removing my heels before slipping my feet into a pair of slides. "What's next?" I ask Liam.

"We have Z100, the Mark Simone Show, and then iHeartRadio," he says, reading from his neatly outlined agenda.

"Great."

"They're all radio, right?" Theo asks from his post by the door.

"Yes," Liam answers him before I can.

"Make them phone in. She's not going into the studios," he says, like he's suddenly in charge of my coming and goings. Although I'm not opposed to the idea, seeing as the last thing I want to do is go and sit in more closed-in spaces, only to be drilled about *the incident.*

"Ah, I'm sorry, but who are you? And why do you think you can come in here and just take charge?" Liam says.

"I'm Theo Valentino, and I don't think I can come in here and take charge. I just did." Theo picks a piece of invisible lint off his impeccable suit, before his eyes meet mine. "Let's go."

Without thought, I push to my feet, pick up my bag, and make my way towards the door.

"Wait, Katy, we need to do these interviews," Liam practically yells at my back.

"Have them call me, Liam. If they want the story, they will," I tell him. I don't usually argue with my manager. I've been following his advice, his itineraries, my whole career. It's worked, and don't get me wrong, he's damn good at his job. Right now, though, all I want to do is get the hell out of here. So that's what I'm doing. I let Theo guide me out of the studio with Amy hot on my heels.

"Does she always follow you everywhere?" Theo asks, gesturing over his shoulder to Amy.

"Yes, it's her job. Also, she's my friend," I say.

"Okay, got it." Theo opens the front door of a black SUV, and I climb in while Amy jumps in the back.

"You know you don't have to come with me." I turn around and tell her.

"And have you go off with Mr. Mafia on your

own? I don't think so," she whispers back, clamping her mouth shut when Theo opens the driver's side door.

"Where are you taking me?" I ask him when he pulls away from the curb.

"Somewhere no one will bother you. You look fucking exhausted," he growls.

"What?" I pull out my compact, opening the mirror. My face is perfectly made up. Not a spec out of place.

"You look fine, but you already know that," Theo says, side-eyeing me.

"Then what gave you the impression I'm exhausted?"

"Your voice, your eyes, your body language. I'm good at reading people," he tells me with a shrug.

"Okay, so where did you say we were going again?"

"I didn't," he answers with his lips tipping up at one side. "You handled yourself really well in that interview."

"I've had a lot of practice," I say, resting my head against the seat, and close my eyes.

Chapter Fourteen

Luca

"**S**it down," Coach grunts, pointing towards the chair opposite his desk. The team manager and assistant coach are standing off to the side. It's never a good thing to be called into the coach's office. It's worse when all three of these fuckers are in here to meet with you.

I sit down, doing my best to mask the fucking pain I'm in. I'm not your typical football player who would be freaking the fuck out in a situation like this. These fuckers can think they're intimidating all day long, but I know none of them would last five minutes in one of our warehouses.

The room is quiet, eerily so, like that quiet when you're about to find out someone died. Which probably isn't too far from the truth. Only it's not someone. It's something. *My career.*

Would I be pissed? You bet. Would I get over it? Eventually.

"There's a lot of noise about what happened yesterday, Valentino. What were you thinking?" Coach asks me.

"That a young woman was going to die if I didn't do something." I shrug my shoulders and furrow my eyebrows. What the fuck did these bastards expect? That I'd stand by and let Katarina die?

"What you did was reckless, but also courageous." This comes from Elliot Hudson, the team manager.

"I did what anyone else would do," I say, blowing off the half-ass compliment.

"No, you did what very few would do." Elliot pins me with a glare.

"Once you meet with the team doctor, we can get a handle on what the plan will be going forward," Coach adds.

"I'm not fired?" I ask.

"No, you're not," Coach says. "You're going to have a rehabilitation program, and hopefully before the seasons up, we'll see you back on the field."

"End of season? Coach, it's a bullet wound. It won't take that long." I smirk.

"I'm not putting you out on that field until we get clearance from *team* doctors, Luca." Coach puts extra emphasis on the word team, meaning I can't attempt to beat the system or pay someone off for a quick signature, or I'll risk ending my career for good.

"Fine, but I'm telling you it won't take that long. I know my body. It heals quick."

"Right, in the meantime, we have some publicity ops for you to do. Your agent will be in touch with offers. They're coming left, right, and center. I'm sure you'll be kept plenty busy."

"I'm not taking any deals," I say. I know a lot of players sell their names to make a quick buck. The thing is my trust fund is larger than anything I'll ever make in the NFL. I don't need additional sponsorships.

"You don't have to take the deals, but we do expect you to do the interviews. There are three lined up for the next few days. You'll have a team rep with you, to prevent you from saying anything that will reflect poorly on the league."

"Interviews? What the fuck for?" I ask.

"You're a hero, Valentino. Everyone wants your story. The incident yesterday stopped our first game of the season. Did you think what you did wouldn't be all over every news channel?"

"No, but why do I need to answer their fucking questions?"

"Because you're the best person to do it. The PR team has been buying you time. According to what we told the press, you're still laid up in the hospital. And if you keep out of sight for the next few days, then that's what they'll continue to believe. Your first appearance is booked for Friday morning. We're working on contacting Kat Star's manager to get you two together for an interview."

"She just had an assassination attempt on her. Don't you think you all should leave her the fuck alone?" I grit my teeth, anger taking over my ability to hold my tongue. I'm not going to let them take advantage of her to line their pockets. Using me is one thing. Using her is off the fucking table.

"She just appeared on GMA this morning. She seems fine. Besides, it's up to her and her team whether or not she wants to appear with you. Now get out of here. Don't be late for that appointment." Coach dismisses me with a wave of his hand.

It's up to her and her team. Like fuck am I going to let her think she has to do these fucking interviews. I know she mentioned having some scheduled, but fuck, does she actually want to do them? Or is it because she's been told she has to?

I make it to the door before coach's voice stops me in my tracks. "Oh, and, Valentino, stay out of sight if you want the paparazzi to give you peace while you recover."

I nod my head. I don't need lessons in dealing

with the paparazzi. I've been doing it my whole life. Once I'm in the car, I send Theo a message.

ME:

How is she?

Placing my phone down on the console, I start the ignition and drive out of the garage. After five minutes, Theo still hasn't replied to my message and I'm getting fucking antsy. Hitting the buttons on the steering wheel, I dial his number.

"I was wondering how long you'd last," he answers the call. "Five minutes, thirty seconds. I'm actually impressed."

"Fuck off. Where is she?"

"Here with me."

"Where's here, Theo?"

"Don't you have a medical appointment to get to?" he says instead.

"How do you know that? Actually, I don't care. I'm on my way to the team's doctors now. Where is Katarina?" I ask more forcefully.

"Hang on," Theo says, and I hear some shuffling.

"Luca?" Katarina's voice fills the car, instantly calming my rattled nerves.

"Hey, bellezza, how are you?" I ask her.

"Good, but I'm not the one who's out and about when they should be in bed. How are you?"

"I'm fine, although I'm not opposed to staying in bed if you're with me." I smirk.

"I'm not sure how much rest and recuperation would happen in that case." She laughs.

"What are you up to?"

"Right now?" she asks.

"Yeah." *Why the fuck are they being so vague?*

"Snooping while I wait for my next radio interview. Your brother made the stations call in, instead of having to go in person. He's a little bossy. Did you know that?" she asks.

"Yeah, I do know that. How are the interviews going?"

"Good, fine, usual…" she replies.

"Bellezza?" I ask.

"Yeah?"

"Where are you and what exactly has you snooping?" I press her.

"Oh, um, Theo brought us to your place. I didn't ask to come here. He didn't actually tell me where we were going until we got here. I can leave. I didn't know. I swear. It's weird, right? I shouldn't be here. I should leave. Also, why do you have a pantry full of chocolate bars? Not that I'm complaining, but surely you can't possibly eat all of those?" Her rambling makes me smile. She's in my house. Snooping, in my house. There really isn't anything incriminating for her to find there. I keep my home turf as clean as a whistle.

"It's fine. Make yourself at home, Katarina. I have an appointment I have to go to, then I'll come find you."

"Okay. Are you sure?" she asks.

"Positive. Can you give the phone back to Theo for a minute? I'll talk to you later."

"Sure," she says.

More shuffling, then my brother's voice comes through the phone. "She's alive and well, Luc," he says.

"I never doubted it." There was a moment when I was legitimately worried, because he hadn't messaged me back right away. But I don't tell him that. "Do me a favor? Keep her out of my gym," I tell him.

"Why? What you got in there?"

"Nothing. I just don't want her in there," I lie. It's the only room in my house that could have her looking at me differently. That's if she were to somehow find her way into the hidden space that's accessed through the gym. The only person who knows it's there is Romeo. That's where I keep my arsenal of weapons. I don't need Katarina going in and seeing that shit. She'd think I'm a fucking sociopath or some shit.

"Uh-huh, I'm going to find out what you're hiding in there, you know."

"There's nothing in there, Theo. I just don't want her hurting herself on the equipment," I tell him. "I gotta go. Just lock the door for me."

"Fine," he grunts, cutting the call just as I pull into the lot outside the doctors' office.

IT TOOK a lot longer meeting with the team doctors than I thought it would. Give me our family physician over those quacks any day. Finally pulling up to my gate, I enter the code. My fingers tap the steering wheel as I wait for the double doors to swing open.

Navigating along the winding driveway, I stop the car at the front of the house. I'm too impatient to wait for the garage doors. I want to get inside as quickly as I can. I called Romeo and Matteo on my way back to the house; they should be here any moment now. I need to see Katarina before I get distracted by their plan to find whoever the fuck is threatening her. I run up the few steps to the front door. When I enter, the place is quiet. Instead of walking through the whole house looking for them, I pull out my phone and open the app that connects me to my security system.

Searching the camera feed, I find Theo creeping around my home gym. I shake my head. I knew he wouldn't be able to help himself. There's not really a reason I haven't shown him or Matteo the secret room. It's just never come up. But seeing as the *not knowing* is killing him, I think I'll hold out a little longer. I scroll through more footage until I find Katarina and her assistant in the theatre room. So I tuck my phone away and head in that direction.

Amy's head pops up in the darkened room. Her finger comes up to her lips as she gestures for me to be quiet. My brows furrow, until I make it through the room, around the front of the seating, and find Katarina passed out on the sofa. "She needs to sleep. I don't think she's been sleeping well the past few weeks," Amy whispers.

"Why not?"

"I think the SFs have upped their level of crazy lately, and then there's all the preparation for the tour. She works a lot," Amy explains.

As many people as I know in the entertainment industry, I've never really given too much thought to how hard they work or what they actually do on a daily basis. I don't know how to help her, how to take away some of her stress.

"What're SFs?" I ask Amy.

"Stalker Fans."

"I don't want her to see that shit anymore. Surely someone else can open her fan mail before she gets to it."

"I can have someone come in and do it, but I'm not sure Katy would approve. She likes being the one to manage the mail. She doesn't want any of her fans to be let down or missed."

"I'll talk to her. She can't be seeing that shit. Fuck, I don't want to see it," I admit, recalling the images Romeo sent me from the mail room. That shit was disturbing, even to me.

"What are your intentions with her?" Amy asks, staring directly at me. She doesn't back down or look away when I give her my best 'don't fuck with me' glare. She's either braver than I gave the little pixie credit for, or she's fucking stupid.

"My intentions? Right now, I intend on carrying

her into my bedroom so she can sleep, while I talk to my brothers about how the fuck we're going to find the asshole who's trying to kill her."

"She hasn't always had everything she has now, and she's worked really hard for what she's earned. I don't want anyone coming in and taking advantage of her," Amy says. "I also don't want to see her get hurt."

"Look around, sweetheart. Does it look like I need to fucking take advantage of whatever she has? And as for hurting her, I'm the one trying to fucking stop that from happening, remember?"

"Okay, but you're not carrying her anywhere. Did you forget the part where you have a hole in your body?" Amy raises her eyebrows in question.

I hate that she's fucking right. There's no way I'm going to be able to lift Katarina and walk with her through the house. I could, but I'd be risking the healing process and injuring myself further. I pull my phone out and text Theo.

ME:

Come to the theatre room.

I fucking hate that I have to ask one of my brother's to carry my girl up to my room for me. I want her comfortable though. I want her sleeping in a bed, not on a theatre recliner.

"You summoned me," Theo says, walking into the room with that cocky gait of his.

"Can you carry Katarina up to my bed? She's asleep," I ask him.

Theo looks from me to Katarina, then back to me. "Sure," he says, and without another word, he bends down, scoops her up, and walks out.

I follow them. Theo places her down on my bed and she stirs, blinking her eyes open. "Mmm, you're not Luca," she mumbles.

"Thank fuck for that," Theo grunts before he straightens his jacket and exits the room.

"Romeo and Matteo are on their way," I tell him as he goes. He waves a hand at me in response.

Chapter Fifteen

Katarina

Luca's voice creeps into my sleep-fogged brain. He's back. I pop my eyes open and see Theo walking out of the bedroom.

"Luca?" I question, looking around the space. *How did I get here? Where is here?* The walls are painted a navy blue, the furniture a dark oak. "How'd I get in bed? And whose bed am I in?" I ask him. Although, if I'm honest, I already know the answer. It's his. I can smell him on the pillow. Would it be weird if I leaned in and sniffed it? Probably…

"You're in my room, my bed. You were asleep." Luca sits on the edge of the mattress, next to where I'm lying.

"Sorry."

"Don't be. Go back to sleep. I'll be downstairs if you need me." He leans over and kisses my forehead.

I know the polite thing to do would be to get up and go home. But right now, the only thing I really want to do is bury myself in these blankets. They're so soft. "Thank you," I say, rolling over and closing my eyes.

THERE'S SHOUTING. I jolt up in bed and my eyes spring open. Why is there shouting? I look around the darkened space. It takes me a minute to remember that I'm in Luca's room. Pulling the blanket aside, I climb off the bed and tiptoe to the door. I can still hear the raised voices. I have no idea what they're yelling about, but I recognize Luca as one of them.

I tiptoe down the stairs, and the voices grow louder and louder the closer I get. My heart hammers in my chest, and I mentally remind myself that I'm safe. It's not him. It's not my father on a drunken tirade. Logically, I know that he can never do that to me again. But logic, fear, and the way my body reacts to outward displays of anger have nothing to do with each other. I find Amy waiting at the bottom of the stairs.

"You okay?" she asks me.

I nod my head. Am I okay? I think I am. Or at least I will be. I just need to get out of here. "Let's go," I tell her, taking hold of her hand as we make our way to the front door undetected. I should thank Luca and Theo for today. And I would... if they weren't currently in a screaming match over God knows what. I just need to go home.

Amy and I walk down the driveway, and the property gates start opening. I don't know if it's luck, or maybe I have an angel looking out for me and things are finally going my way.

"Maybe we should call an Uber," I suggest, and Amy begins tapping on her phone.

A black SUV pulls to a stop in front of us not even a minute later. My steps freeze. Amy grips my hand and gives it a reassuring squeeze. When the back passenger door opens, a pair of shiny black dress shoes step out onto the gravel, and Luca's dad pins us with a look I don't quite recognize. Removing the sunglasses from his face, he tilts his head as his eyes narrow in on us.

"Are you going somewhere?" he asks.

"Home," I say.

"And how exactly do you plan on getting there?"

I don't know why, but there's an authority to him that makes me want to answer all of his questions without argument. "Ah, an Uber?"

"Did my son make you leave alone?" he questions, adjusting the sleeves of his shirt and jacket while glancing behind me at the house.

"Um, no. I just... I need to go home," I tell him.

Mr. Valentino looks at me silently for what seems like forever before he nods his head towards his car. "Get in. I'll give you a lift."

Amy squeezes my hand again, and I glance at her. "Are you sure we should be doing that?"

I don't know why, but I trust this family. It's weird, and I'm not sure I have the energy to unpack why I feel like I can trust them when all evidence points to their ongoing criminal activity. Then again, I've come to learn that has little to do with someone's actual character. Just look at Zane?

"It's okay. Come on. I just want to go home," I tell her. Thankfully Amy follows me into the back of the car, and Mr. Valentino climbs in after us.

"Where to, boss?" The big, burly driver asks, while another man in the front passenger seat turns around to look at us.

"What's the address, Katarina?" Mr. Valentino questions me.

I rattle off the information, and the driver reverses out of the gates. "Thank you, Mr. Valentino, you really didn't have to do this," I tell him.

"You can call me T. And, yes, I did. I can't have you out on the streets alone. Did you forget the part where someone is trying to kill you?" he asks as he types something out on his phone.

"It's not easy to forget," I mumble.

"It seems my son has a vested interest in keeping you alive. I imagine once he finds you're not wherever it was he last left you, he's going to be beyond worried."

Well, way to make me feel bad for leaving without saying anything. "I…" I let my sentence trail off. I'm not sure what to say to that.

"They were all arguing about something to do with an armory when we left," Amy says.

"An armory?" Mr. Valentino asks.

"Well, that's what it sounded like. They're loud and talk really fast." She shrugs.

"Try living with them." Mr. Valentino chuckles.

My phone vibrates in my pocket. Pulling it out, I see an unknown number plastered across the screen. I don't answer numbers I don't know, so I hit decline. Mr. Valentino's phone rings a second later.

"Luca, have you lost something?" he answers.

"Yeah, my fucking girlfriend. Where are you taking her?" Luca's response can be heard from where I'm sitting, because he's that loud.

Girlfriend? I look to Amy, confused. She shrugs. "I think he's a little batshit crazy, Katy. Why would he think you're his girlfriend?" she whispers.

"I have no idea," I tell her, although I can feel the blush that creeps up my neck as I recall the events of the night before. Surely, one hot, passionate night together does not make for girlfriend status. Maybe he's talking about someone else, and I'm totally getting carried away in my own thoughts. If that's the case, that means what we did last night should never have happened. And I really want it to happen again.

"Girlfriend? Son, you do know you can't just pluck a girl out and claim her as yours. Does she have any idea you've decided this relationship status?" Mr. Valentino asks into the phone while looking at me.

"Pops, just tell me where you're taking her. Please. Or better yet, hand her the phone."

"Fine, hold on." Mr. Valentino lowers the device from his ear to pass it to me. "It's for you," he says, one side of his mouth tipping up at the corner, and in that moment, I can see where his sons get their looks from.

I take the phone and raise it to my ear. "Hello?"

"Katarina, where are you going? Why'd you leave? And why the fuck didn't you come and tell me you were going?" he asks.

"First of all, you, Luca Valentino, are not my keeper. I don't need to inform you of my comings and goings. Second, you were busy arguing with your brothers when I left. I'm going home, by the way. You know, that big ol' house I paid a whole bunch of money for. It's where I live, and your dad was kind enough to offer me a ride."

"You shouldn't be alone," he says.

"I'm not. I'm with Amy."

"You need actual protection, Katarina."

"Okay, look, I appreciate your concern. But I'm

fine. I really am too tired for this, Luca. Can we discuss it later?"

"I'm sorry. I just… want to keep you safe. That's all. I'll talk to you soon, okay? Pass the phone back to Pops."

I return the device to Mr. Valentino, who puts it to his ear and listens to whatever Luca says. I can't hear him this time. He's quieter. "Of course," his dad replies and ends the call.

Chapter Sixteen

Luca

She left. Just walked out and I didn't even fucking notice. It was my gate alarm ringing through the house that finally gave me pause. When I logged on to see who it was, I watched Katarina climb into the back of my father's car. I should give her the space that she wants. But I don't know how to do that. I've asked Pops to stay at her place until I get there. I won't be far behind them.

"I gotta go," I tell all three of my brothers, who

are staring at me like I've grown another head. "What?" I ask them.

"Since when do you have girlfriends?" Romeo asks.

"Since now. It's not like any of you fuckers can talk. I watched each of you fall at the feet of your wives the minute you met." I point at them one by one.

"Technically, I was six years old when I met my wife. I highly doubt I fell at Savvy's feet or that you remember when I met her, considering you were a baby," Matteo replies.

"He might not have been old enough to remember, but I was, and you didn't just fall at her feet, bro. You rolled over and played dead." Theo laughs.

"Whatever, I'm out." I spin on my heel and exit the living room.

"Wait! I'll come with." Romeo jogs to catch up with me.

The other two don't follow us. I know they'll both be doing their best to get into that armory in my gym that Theo somehow fucking found, despite my best efforts. I don't know how the fuck he figured it out. What he couldn't do was actually get past the locked door. I know he called Romeo for help, to which my twin played dumb.

"How long do you think it'll take them?" Romeo asks from the passenger seat of my car, referencing the coded lock.

I laugh. "Long enough to give them the shits." I smile.

I don't give two fucks if they see the armory. They are more than welcome to whatever I have in there anyway. It's more the game of me knowing something those two don't that I'm playing at. I have no doubt they'll waste their time breaking into the door. I actually wish I was there to watch the look on their faces when they do get inside and see the collection I've amassed without their knowledge.

It's been a hobby of sorts, to seek out rare guns and knives from around the world. I'm surprised Theo hasn't already caught on to the fact I've been buying the shit. He's just like my pops in so many ways. Nothing really seems to get past either of them.

"How're Matilda and Livvy?" I ask Romeo, changing the subject.

"Beautiful," he answers.

I roll my eyes. Of course they're beautiful. I could have told him that. I lived with Livvy and Romeo all throughout college, right up to the point Liv got knocked up and they decided to go out on their own.

"What's the plan here, Luca? You just gonna barge your way into this woman's life and hope she keeps you around?"

"Can't be worse than planting listening devices in the library where she studies," I throw back at him, reminding him of how he and his wife came to be. My brother listened to Liv's conversations for weeks before he got up the courage to actually go and talk to her.

"Why'd she sneak out?" Romeo asks.

"No idea, but I plan to find out." So I can prevent it from ever happening again.

Theo and Romeo went through all of the fucked-up fan mail last night. They've culled it down to three suspects. The worst of the worst, according to Theo. That's where we're starting our search. I want them all to fucking die, and I plan on making them disappear. Anyone who thinks they have some sick fucking claim to Katarina needs to be eliminated. I really don't care if I have to spend the rest of my life taking these motherfuckers out.

I get she's not going to give up her job anytime soon, and I wouldn't want her to. I just want her to be safe. I don't want sick fucks out there trying to get at her. I always knew the world was full of psychopaths —fuck, I would have put myself in that category as well. Until I saw the shit that was being sent to Katarina. The amount of death threats she's received, from whom we've determined appear to be three different men, is like something out of a horror movie. According to one of them, she's a demon, because nobody that perfect can be human. Therefore, she must be sacrificed to save the good of mankind. It's fucked up. Although I do agree that she's perfect, because she is.

"You know, maybe you should just have some guys stay at her house tonight and give her the space she wants. Come back to my place and hang with Liv and me," Romeo suggests.

"Maybe. I want to see her first though," I tell him, having no intention of leaving her side once I get there. I'm still fucking pissed that she managed to get out of my house without me knowing. Pulling into her driveway, I enter the new key code into her gate and park up behind my pops's car. Leo and Don are standing outside.

"Boys." Leo nods at us. He's been our father's driver for around ten years now.

"Leo, how is he?" I ask, referring to my old man. Leo has become an expert on his moods.

"Amused." Leo answers with a smirk.

I roll my eyes. Of course he's amused by my downfall. I was the last one standing. I swore off love. Made claims of remaining the eternal bachelor. Not that I'm in love now. That'd be insane. What I'm *in* is fucking lust. I want Katarina something fierce. It's not love.

I let myself into her house. The door should be locked. Not that a locked door could keep me out if I wanted in. Pops is standing in the foyer with a pissed-off looking Zane. I thought he left—at least that's the message I got from Theo. I glance between my father and the biker. Katarina isn't with them, so instead of approaching them, I make my way upstairs to her bedroom. I have no idea where she is, but this is the first place I thought to look.

Thank god I don't have to walk the halls of the

entire house. Before I even enter her room, I can hear her voice. The melody she's singing has my arms breaking out in goose bumps. I've heard her songs more than once—you'd have to be living under a rock not to—but this is different. She's singing "Amazing Grace," her voice echoing off the bathroom walls as she harmonizes. I stand in the doorway and lean against the frame.

Have you ever felt like you're in the presence of greatness? That's what I'm feeling right now as I silently watch Katarina.

She's in the shower, and not even the noise of the running water drowns out her vocals. Her eyes are closed as she tilts her head slightly upwards. I could listen to her sing like this forever. It's evident in her posture, her calmness, that she's connecting with the lyrics. The song washes over me, blanketing me in everything that is her.

"*How precious did that grace appear, the hour I first believed.*"

I close my eyes with memories of just two days ago when I saw her standing on the field, a gold microphone in hand and a smile that had me captivated the second I bore witness to her beauty. And then the red dot. The image of that fucking red dot still sends my blood cold. Opening my eyes, I realize she's stopped singing.

"Are you okay?" she asks me, not doing a single thing to cover her naked body from my view as she turns the shower off and steps out.

"I was enjoying the show." I smirk.

"The singing or the showering?"

"Both," I tell her.

"You know that's creepy, right?" she says.

"If you think that's creepy, then you probably don't want to know the thoughts I have in my head." I can't help but frown when she wraps a big white towel around herself.

"Sometimes mystery goes a long way in a relationship, Luca. Maybe you should keep those thoughts to yourself... for now."

"You know, my pops said I can't just claim that you're my girlfriend. Apparently I'm supposed to ask you if you wanna be or some shit." I shrug.

She laughs. "Are you asking me to be your girlfriend, Luca? Because I gotta be honest. If that's how you ask girls out, I'm not sure how you've ever managed to have any girlfriends at all."

"I haven't ever had a girlfriend. I've never met anyone I wanted to spend more than one night with."

"What makes me different?"

"Well, for one, my cock fucking loves you. He's addicted already. Just hearing your voice has me hard, bellezza. And two, I honestly have no fucking idea why you're different. I just know that I want to get to know you. I want to be around you as much as humanly possible."

"Huh." Katarina walks past me into her bedroom. I watch as she disappears into the closet.

"What does *huh* mean?" I ask, following her like the lost fucking puppy I am.

"I don't know what you want me to say, Luca. I don't have an easy life. I'm busy. I'm a lot to handle. I don't think you really know what you're getting yourself into, wanting to date me."

"Bellezza, I'm more than ready to dive into this with you. Whatever comes our way, we can deal with it. I'm not exactly a prize catch. I know that. Dating me comes with its own set of challenges. Trust me, whatever deal breakers you think you have, I'm one hundred percent certain mine are worse."

"For the past four years, I've done everything I'm supposed to do. Everything to get me to where I am today with my career. Why is it that after knowing you for just two days, I feel like being reckless all of a sudden?"

I smile. "Babe, reckless is my middle name."

Chapter Seventeen

Katarina

I'm not sure I can be as reckless as Luca. If I could, I'd most certainly want to be. My eyes travel up and down his body as he leans a shoulder on the doorframe. He's wearing a pair of grey sweats and a white shirt. Nothing special, yet somehow he makes it look like he should be on a runway in Paris. Whatever they've got in the water over at the Valentino household, it's working for them. I haven't seen one person who doesn't look like they've been molded to perfection. Not one ugly duckling amongst them, despite what Romeo claims.

Averting my eyes, I reach for a skirt and then find a light-pink blouse and pull it from the hanger.

"Wait," Luca says, walking farther into the room.

"What?" I ask, confused. Before I know what's happening, his hands are on my hips, walking me backwards until my spine presses against the island counter that houses some of my favorite handbags. Luca's arm swipes out, shoving the bags aside, and I gasp as I watch a blue Hermès bag fall to the floor. "Luca, those are worth a ton. You can't just throw them on the floor." I try to get out of his hold to grab it.

Luca tightens his grip on me, picking me up and sitting me on top of the island. "I'll buy you a new one," he says before his fingers come up to my towel, where I have it folded above my breasts. "I can't waste this opportunity," he says, tugging at the plush material.

"What opportunity?" I ask, looking down as the towel falls away from my body, leaving me completely exposed to him.

"The you being naked kind," he says, running the tips of two fingers down the middle of my chest, past my belly button. My back arches as he reaches my clit, and those fingers waste no time finding my slick entrance and pushing inside. "Fuck me, you're wet."

"I did just shower," I moan as he withdraws his fingers and then pushes them back in.

"Way to bruise my ego, bellezza. Here I was, thinking you were wet for me." Luca's lips graze down the side of my neck.

"You might have a little to do with it." My words are breathless as he increases the pace of his movements. Just as I feel like I'm going to fly over the edge of ecstasy, Luca pulls his hand away. I blink my eyes open and watch as he brings those two fingers to his mouth and sucks them.

"Fucking hell," he groans before dropping to his knees and yanking my legs apart as wide as they'll go. His tongue is lapping at my sensitive clit and I'm back there, on that edge of the cliff, within seconds. "I want it all. Give it all to me, bellezza." He pulls away, looking up at me expectantly.

"Well, don't stop then!" Taking hold of the back of his head, I push him onto my mound. He doesn't put up a fight, thankfully. His mouth latches on to my clit and he sucks, sending me over that edge I was desperately seeking. I come, screaming out God knows what, as whatever words spill from my lips are completely unrecognizable to my ears.

Luca licks at my slit until the last of the shakes leave my body, and I'm nothing more than a worn-out pile of limbs. I don't have the energy to move. Then he stands, gripping my chin between his fingers, and his mouth slams down over mine, his tongue pushing its way inside. I can taste myself on him, which oddly isn't as bad as I thought it might be.

Wrapping my legs over his hips, I tug him against

me, locking my feet together behind his back. My arms close around his neck as I hold him tighter. I can't seem to get close enough. No matter how much of my body is pressed up against his, it's not enough. I want more. I want to get closer.

"I want you," I tell him, pulling away from his kiss.

"You have me," he says, leaning in again.

I shake my head. Unwrapping my arms from his neck, I let my hands run over his shoulders, down his rock-hard pecs, and past the ridges and grooves of his stomach. I reach the top of his sweats, dipping my hand under the band and slipping my fingers inside his boxers before grabbing his cock. "This… I want this," I tell him. Using my other hand, I pull his sweats and boxers down enough to free his shaft. My hand tightens as I pump it up and down the smooth skin, my thumb swiping the precum off the tip of his cock and rubbing it along the length of him.

"It's all yours, bellezza. Where do you want it?"

"What do you mean where do I want it? I want it inside me, Luca." I increase my speed.

He hisses, his jaw tightens, and his body becomes more rigid. "Where do you want it, bellezza? As in you have three choices, your pussy, your mouth, or your ass?" He leans in and whispers the words into my ear before nibbling on the bottom of the lobe.

"Oh god." My back arches into him. "Every-where… I want it everywhere," I tell him. "No, I want it in my pussy right now." I pull his tip closer to my entrance. As soon as he's lined up, Luca takes hold of my hips, tilting them up slightly, and thrusts inside me, bottoming out. "Oh fuck." My legs tense around his waist, and my hands cling to his shoulders in an attempt to stay upright.

"You're so fucking tight, so fucking good," Luca grunts as he slowly pulls out before thrusting back in again, hitting that magic spot he seems to have a damn map for.

"Yes. That, keep doing that," I tell him, releasing his shoulders, and I fall back until I'm flat on the island.

Luca's hands squeeze at my ass as he picks me up and drives into me harder and faster. This angle is deeper than before. He's hitting an all new high. I'm so wet I can hear the sloshing sound my pussy is making with each of his thrusts. "You should see how fucking beautiful you are, bellezza. Stunning. I've never seen anything more breathtaking than how you look right now. How your pussy looks taking all of my cock."

My legs are still around his waist, squeezing as tight as I can to hold on to him. Luca brings one of his hands to the flat of my stomach, and his fingers travel south until he finds my clit and rubs small, soft circles. I arch my hips up, seeking more friction. I need it. I'm so close to a second orgasm. Which, let's be honest, up until last night, I thought the whole multiple orgasms thing was a myth.

Newsflash. It's not.

"Yes. I..." My eyes shut. My whole body is covered in a light sheen of sweat as it shakes with the explosive orgasm that overtakes me. Luca rips his cock free, and I open my eyes just as he pumps his seed all over my stomach. "I think, when I can walk again, I'm gonna need to retake that shower," I say between panted breaths.

"I'll join you, but you have to sing for me while we're in there."

"You want me to sing to you?" I ask, surprised.

"You have the voice of an angel, Katarina. I want to hear you sing just as much as I want to fuck you. Which is a fucking lot if you're wondering." He smirks.

"Well, I can't say I've ever been given a compliment like that before." I smile.

"If anyone else tells you they want to fuck you, I'm going to kill them." His tone hardens, and I have the feeling that he's dead serious.

I blink up at him. I don't know what to say to that, except I do. "Well, if anyone says they want to fuck you, feel free to kill them too. Because as much as I'd like to say I would do it, I know myself and I couldn't. But I also wouldn't feel bad if the bitches disappear. You should know I'm an only child and I never learned to share."

"Bellezza, there is no sharing happening in this relationship of ours."

"You know, I haven't agreed to the whole girl-friend thing yet." I raise an eyebrow in question.

"Your pussy just choked the fuck out of my cock. She agreed for you."

"She? Please tell me you are not referring to parts of my anatomy as a *she*." I scrunch up my face. I don't think I like that.

"She..." Luca says, running his fingers through my wet folds. "...likes me very much." He shrugs.

"*She* just likes being petted," I moan as he shoves two fingers inside me. Surely, I can't actually be ready to go another round. What is it about Luca Valentino that's turned me into a wanton mess?

Chapter Eighteen

Luca

I leave Katarina in her closet to get dressed and head downstairs. It's oddly quiet in the foyer where I left Romeo to deal with Pops and that fucking biker friend of hers. I do, however, find Amy who appears around a corner with an arm full of bags.

"Need a hand?" I ask her.

She pauses midstep, her eyes bugging out of her head. "Ah, no, I'm fine."

"Why do you look like you were just caught with your hand in the cookie jar?" I ask her.

"Well, it's not every day we have half-naked men roaming the halls of this house." She doesn't make eye contact with me as she says this.

"Sorry, my shirt got destroyed." I smirk.

Apparently, going for a quickie with fresh sutures doesn't bode well for a white shirt. I started bleeding through the bandages and onto the fabric. Katarina applied new dressings without batting an eyelash. I've yet to press her on her epic first aid skills. She didn't get squeamish at the sight of my wounds, or the blood. She did, however, chastise me for being reckless with my self-care. I then informed her that I'd tear every last stitch out and still want to fuck her. A little blood isn't going to stop me from getting to sink my cock into her.

"Your entourage is in the blue living room. Head towards the kitchen, take the hall on the left, and then turn right. I'm sure you'll hear them long before you find them," Amy says and rushes off.

Following her directions, I make my way through this gigantic fucking house. Really, it's overkill, and I grew up in a home bigger than this one. I eventually come to the *blue* living room. As soon as I step inside, it becomes apparent why it's called that. The space is covered in all shades of blue, right down to the very blue pastel carpet. There's a sofa set, a three-seater, and a two seater, all full of white and blue cushions. Then there's a single chair in the back corner of the room. It's dark, almost denim in color, and the fabric appears well worn, like someone sits in it a lot. Taking my eyes off everything blue, I turn my attention to my pops and brother, who seem to be looking through some shit that's spread out on the coffee table. Zane stands on the other side of them doing the same, his mouth pinched with a frown.

"She can't see this. We need to get rid of it, get it out of this fucking room. If she sees this... in this room..." Zane's sentence trails off when his eyes meet mine. "Where's Kat?" he asks me.

"Getting dressed." I can't help but smirk as I say the words. Judging by the death glare the bastard gives me, he realizes the meaning.

Yeah, fucker, I just left her naked and thoroughly exhausted.

"You need to keep her from coming in here," he says. "We need to get this out without her seeing it."

"What the fuck are you talking about?" I ask, walking farther into the room.

Pops steps towards me with a hand out in a stop motion. "Luc, you don't need to see this. Just take Katarina to your place, or mine. Get her out of the house," he says.

Yeah, that's not *going to make me not want to see it any less.*

I side-step my old man and take the few extra paces to get a glimpse of what they're looking at. I pause, blinking a couple of times, because even I can't fathom what the fuck I'm looking at. It's a full-size doll. Not just a doll. It's Katarina's twin. A replica.

The doll is naked, and covered in what appear to be cuts and bruises. What makes my blood run cold is the left arm. Sliced open with what I fucking hope is fake blood dripping out. There's a message written across the span of the stomach.

Useless piece of shit! You should have done it right the first time. But don't worry. I'll ensure you don't make that mistake again.

"What the fuck?" I hiss between clenched teeth. "I'm going to fucking kill them. I want this fucker now!" I scream.

"Bro, calm down. We'll find him. Leo is scanning the video surveillance of the room as we speak. He'll find the fucker who put this shit here, and then it's only a matter of time till we get him."

"How do you find a ghost?" Zane asks, shaking his head, his eyes glued to the doll.

"What are you talking about?"

"Those words. It's what her father used to say to her. But it can't be him."

"Why?" I ask. I don't know anything about Katarina's family yet, but if her father speaks to her like *that*, he won't be speaking at all for much fucking longer.

"Because I killed him when we were sixteen," Zane says.

Well, fuck, I really wanted to hate the guy.

"Does she know that?" I ask him.

"She knows that he died in a car accident," Zane says.

So that would be a no. She has no idea her best friend killed her father. I'm not sure how she'd feel about that knowledge either.

"You killed him?" The voice from behind me has me spinning on my feet.

Guess we're all about to find out exactly what she thinks...

"Kat... I... it's not..." Zane stutters, clearly at a loss for words.

"Babe, I'm hungry. Let's go eat." I walk up to her and attempt to turn her around. I don't particularly want her to see what else is in this room.

"What? You know where the kitchen is, Luca. I'm not your mother," Katarina says before looking past me to Zane. "You, outside, now." She points at him, spins around, and stomps off.

I glance over my shoulder at Zane, who looks like he'd rather be doing anything other than going outside with Katarina right now. "Fuck!" he hisses under his breath. "Someone get rid of this shit. I fucking hoped I'd never have to see *that* again," he says.

"What do you mean *again?*" I step in front of him, blocking his attempt to flee.

"Who do you think found her in the shitty little bathroom, passed out with her wrists split open?" he says. "Because it sure as fuck wasn't her piece of shit father." He brushes past me, exiting the room.

I'm about to follow Zane out the door, only to be stopped by Leo walking in. "Did you find anything?" I ask him.

"Got a face. I've sent it through to Danny to run facial rec," he says, handing me a piece of paper. I turn it over and stare at the fucker whose breaths are numbered. I wouldn't say I particularly enjoy killing. I do it because I have to. But I can already tell this time is going to be different.

Chapter Nineteen

Katarina

I should have suspected it. Why didn't I ever think of the specifics of how my father crashed into that tree?

Except I know why. I was so overwhelmed with relief when I found out he died I didn't question anything. I simply followed whatever instructions Zane gave me in order to stay out of the foster care system.

He killed him. Zane killed my dad. For me. The

guilt of what he's done, because of our friendship, is a lot to handle right now. I'm sitting on the swing seat on the back patio that overlooks the pool. The water shimmers along the surface. Inviting me. Taunting me. Maybe I should just jump in and forget everything else. Water seems to be my calming zone. The bath, the shower, the pool. Any body of water really. I find whenever I submerge myself in water, all my worries float away. I can just forget. In fact, the bath is where I've written most of my songs.

Ironic, considering how many terrible memories it holds too. But I won't delve into the grim nature of my mother's death today. I can only deal with one deceased parent at a time.

If I didn't have to face Zane right now and find out why he's lied to me for the past seven years, then I would probably just jump right in.

"Kat?" Zane's voice is soft as he slides the back door open.

"I don't know if I want to hug you or hit you over the head with a really heavy rock right now," I tell him when he comes to a stop in front of me.

"I'll take option one." He smirks, sitting himself down beside me.

"We promised. When we were eight years old, we promised to never lie to each other, Zane. How many other lies have you told me?" I ask him.

"Technically, I didn't lie. I told you your dad died in a crash. He did. Physically, he was inside the wreck. I just left out the part about how I caused it…"

"How?"

"I cut his break lines," he says. "He didn't die from the impact, though. I followed him that night. When the car collided with the tree, I went to make sure. He was still alive. So I... I shot him, Kat. And I'm really fucking sorry if I hurt you, but I'd do it again."

"I hate that I made you do that," I say.

"You didn't make me do anything. I did it because I chose you. He was going to kill you. We both knew it would happen eventually."

"Probably."

"I'll leave if you want me to, Kat." Zane sounds broken.

"I don't hate you. I appreciate everything you've done for me, Zane. I just wish there was a way I could pay you back."

"You don't owe me anything—although there is something you could do for me," he says.

"What?" I ask, curious. Zane has never asked me for anything before.

"You could keep your boyfriend and his family in there from killing me." His lips tip up into a grin.

"Luca's not going to kill you." I roll my eyes.

"You don't know that family like I do, Kat."

"I don't know them at all," I admit.

"Look, I've never told you who you can and can't date," Zane starts, and I can't help but laugh. "Okay, maybe I've tried to tell ya once or twice," he says.

"Once or twice," I parrot and laugh again.

"That's not the point. I'm not going to tell you not to date him. I'm going to beg you to open your eyes and really think about what it means to get involved with the Valentinos."

"You know, if people judged everyone by their families, I'd be up shit creek."

"It's not the same. Luca is one of them, Kat. Don't think for a minute he's not every bit as dangerous as the rest of them."

"I don't know what you're talking about. I'm dating a football player." I give him my press-practiced smile.

"It's fucking scary how good you are at lying," Zane says with a shake of his head. His phone rings just as he opens his mouth to say something else. "Hold that thought." He stands and pulls his cell from the top pocket of his leather vest. "Babe, everything okay?" he answers. I can't hear what Marcia is saying on the other line, but I do hear the panic in Zane's reply. "Shit, I'll be there. I'm leaving now." He pockets the phone again and looks at me with a torn expression.

"What's wrong?" I ask him.

"Marcia's in labor."

"Well, what the hell are you doing still standing here. Go!" I shout, jumping up from the swing and shoving him towards the door.

"What about you?"

"I'll be fine. But Marcia really will kill you if you don't get to her before that baby pops out," I tell him.

"Come with me."

"I can't. I'm sorry, Zane. I just…" I shake my head. I haven't been back to our shitty little hometown since I left. And the hospital…? Yeah, there is no way I can go there and not be bombarded by the memories of endless broken bones, cuts, and bruises that I had to have patched up in the ER. Or the images of my mother sobbing to a social worker, only to go right back to my father the same day.

"I know. I'm sorry. I don't like leaving you here when some crazy motherfucker is trying to get to you." He wraps his arms around me and squeezes.

"Did you miss the new security system I've had installed? I'll be fine," I assure him, returning his hug.

"Promise me you'll listen to Luca. I might not like the bastard, but I know he has the means to keep you safe."

"I *like* him. Plus he's really, really good at—"

Zane's palm covers my mouth, stopping me midsentence. "Do not finish that, Kat. I don't want to know," he says and drops his hand.

"I was going to say *football*," I tell him with a shrug. I reach out and push him towards the door again. "You really need to go and catch my new niece or nephew.

"Fuck, right. Call me if anything happens," Zane yells as he runs through the house and past a pissed-off looking Luca, who is leaning against the back door. What is it with this guy and leaning on doorways, and how the hell does he make that stance look so damn delectable? If it weren't for the darkness in his eyes, I'd probably go jump him right now.

Instead, I read his tense body language, his clenched jaw that's developed a little tick, and step backwards. I glance to my left and then my right, looking for the best way to get around him. To get away from him. I don't realize that I've continued to back away until my spine hits the railing. It's a learned reaction. I feel like I'm on autopilot, moving with muscle memory.

Luca's face changes. He appears almost hurt as he takes measured steps towards me. "Katarina?" he questions. I don't answer. All I can do is watch as he slowly closes the gap between us. "You're scared," he whispers as he stops right in front of me.

I shake my head. I can't tell him. I can't tell him how fucked up I am from my childhood.

"I don't like this look on your beautiful face. I don't ever want you to be scared. Especially of me. I'm the last person on earth who would ever hurt you."

"I'm sorry," I say. I don't mean to be scared of him. And if I really put thought into it, I'm not. I'm scared of the unknown. What if he does flip out? What if I do something that sets him off?

"Come here." Luca's arms wrap around my shoulders, and my body is pulled up against his. My hands meet the bare skin of his chest. "You don't have to be sorry. I just need to know what I did to scare you so I don't fucking do it again."

"It's not you," I tell him. "I'm just easily freaked out when it comes to men," I admit.

"What freaks you out?"

I take a huge breath. "Yelling… I don't like yelling," I tell him.

"Okay, what else?"

I pull back and peer up at him. All I see in his eyes right now is concern, worry. "You looked angry," I say.

He blinks a few times. "I'm sorry. I wasn't angry with you."

"Who were you angry at?"

"Your friend had his filthy hands all over you," he says. "I don't like it."

"He hugged me. He wasn't groping me, Luca."

"I know. Still don't like it."

"Why didn't you just say something?" I ask him.

"I might not like it, but I'm not an idiot. I'm also not trying to control you. I won't tell you who you can and can't be friends with, bellezza," he says. "Unless they're Russian. We are *not* on good terms with the Russians," he quickly adds with a smirk.

"I can't even tell if that's meant to be a joke or not." I laugh.

"Come on, we've gotta go." Luca closes his hand around mine and leads me back into the house.

"Where are we going?" I ask.

"I made dinner reservations."

I stop, forcing his steps to halt. "What? I can't go

out for dinner. It'll be a paparazzi nightmare. They'll be everywhere."

"Are you worried about being seen with me?" he asks.

"No, not at all. I'm worried that I'll do something that'll end up spread across every tabloid."

"Come on, I'll make sure there are no paparazzi," he assures me.

"You seriously have a god complex," I tell him.

"That's probably because I keep hearing you call me a god."

"I've never called you a god."

"I'm one hundred percent certain it was you screaming out 'oh god' when I was eating your pussy less than two hours ago."

My whole face heats with the memory. I can't really argue with his reasoning, even if it is farfetched. So, instead, I follow Luca to the car. It's not until I'm sliding inside that I remember I'm not dressed to go out in public...

Chapter Twenty

Luca

As soon as I pull out of Katarina's estate, I dial Matteo's number. He takes a while to pick up. When he does, I can hear the sound of the kids squealing in the background. My brother has two boys: Lorenzo is two and Enzo is seven months old. "Shh, Zio Luc is on the phone," Matteo says in a softened tone before turning the asshole version on me. "What do you want?"

"I need you to put some road blocks out. Two in every direction from Joe's on Broadway."

"You're joking, right?" He laughs.

"Nope."

"Why? It better be good, Luc. It's fucking Broadway. You realize that's going to take a lot of fucking effort," he huffs.

"Look, if you can't do it, that's fine. I'll call Theo," I say, knowing it'll get him to agree quicker. Matteo won't ever admit that Theo is better than him at anything. He's always competing with our eldest brother, looking to beat him at whatever he can. The only thing he's never been interested in besting him at has been Theo's position in the family. None of us want to be the next Don. I don't think Theo even really wants it. Not that he'd admit that to anyone.

"Don't be stupid. Of course I can do it. I just want to know why," he says.

"I'm taking Katarina for pizza, and she'd prefer the paparazzi didn't find out about it," I tell him.

"See? If you'd opened with that, we could have skipped all of this useless conversation. You should have just said it's for Katarina."

"The fact I was asking for a favor should have been enough," I counter.

"Meh, it should, but Kat Star holds more weight than you do, bro. Sorry, but it is what it is." He laughs before he cuts the call without saying goodbye.

"We're going for pizza?" Katarina asks from the passenger seat.

"Not just pizza, the best pizza in New York City, babe." Reaching over, I take hold of her palm and entwine my fingers with hers before placing our joined hands on my thigh.

"Pizza's not on the approved foods list," she says so quietly I almost think I'm hearing things.

"Who made this bullshit list for you?"

"The dieticians. Why?"

"Because I'm gonna kill them. They're idiots. You can eat pizza, eat as much of it as you want. And if you really want to work off the calories later—not that you need to—I can think of plenty of ways we could work out together."

"I don't remember the last time I ate anything that wasn't on the list..." Her voice sounds almost wistful.

"Well, lucky for you, I'm an expert at breaking the rules. Stick with me, bellezza, and you'll be a rebel in no time."

Katarina smiles a huge, wide smile that lights up her entire face. "I guess if I'm going to start breaking rules, I might as well do it with a pro, right?"

"Right," I agree.

Thirty minutes later, we're stopping as I pull up to the barricade my brother somehow managed to get set up two blocks from Joe's. Pressing the button, I wind down my window. I have no idea who the guy standing guard at the barricade is, but he takes one look at me before nodding his head and speaking into the earpiece he's wearing.

"Go on through," he says to me with a wave of his arm.

"Thanks." I roll the window back up. I look across to find Katarina ducked down low in her seat. "What are you doing?" I ask her.

"I don't want to be photographed," she says.

Glancing out the windshield, I can see a crowd of paparazzi gathered around the perimeter of the barricade. "Fucking pigs," I hiss through my teeth. "Bellezza, they can't see you in here. It's tinted glass, babe, and it's two shades darker than legal," I tell her with a grin.

"Oh." She sits up again and straightens her hair.

"You know you're lucky my ego isn't easily bruised, because this whole not wanting to be photographed with me thing would really cut a guy down. If that guy wasn't me, of course."

Without saying anything, she takes her phone out of her pocket. And when I pull up in front of Joe's, she unclips her seat belt. "Kiss me," she says.

I don't have to be told twice. I'll kiss her all fucking day, any day of the week. My hand cups her cheek as our mouths meet. Darting my tongue out, I lick the seam of her lips, parting them. My tongue delves inside her mouth, and I'm about to take this kiss further, by picking her up and tugging her over the center console to straddle me, when I see the flash. Pulling away, ready to murder some fucker who got through the barricade, I see her phone up in the air.

She snapped a picture of us kissing, and I can't hold back my grin.

"One more. Smile," she says, raising and angling the device before pressing her face against mine and taking a selfie. She smiles that big, wide, genuine smile —the one she doesn't wear that often. Because it's real and not rehearsed. I can't help but stare in awe at her as she clicks a dozen or so more images.

"I'm posting this to Insta, and I'm tagging you. Don't say I didn't warn you." She smirks as she taps away at her screen. When she's finished, my phone pings with a notification. I open it to see that she's posted two photos. One of me staring at her in awe and one of us kissing.

The caption reads: *A reckless faith on an uncharted sea. A new beginning that hopefully never ends.*

I hit the like button and reply with: *She's out of my league, but I'm keeping her anyway.*

Katarina reads the comment on her phone and smiles. "I'm so not out of your league, Luca, and this whole keeping her thing—yeah, we need to work on your belief that I'm something you can possess."

"You have no idea how much I want to possess your body right now," I tell her, my eyes landing on her exposed cleavage. She's wearing a white V-neck shirt and a pair of denim cutoffs. How the hell she makes something so simple look so fucking amazing, I have no idea.

"You promised me the best pizza in New York.

Let's go before I change my mind and make you take me to a salad bar."

My face scrunches up in disgust. "The words *salad* and *bar* do not belong together," I say, climbing out of the car. Scanning the surroundings as I make my way to her door, I stop when I see some creepy-looking fucker staring from a window in the building opposite us. He doesn't move, doesn't blink, just stares. Not at me. I follow his line of sight. He's staring at the passenger side door of my fucking car. The door I was about to open for Katarina.

I pull my phone out of my pocket and call my dad. I don't have a good feeling about this guy at all, and there is no way in hell I'm going to let her out of the car. Turning around, I walk back to the driver's side with my phone to my ear.

Come on, answer the fucking phone. I silently curse out my old man for not answering quickly enough, climb into the car, and start the ignition. "Put your seat belt back on." My voice is strained, harsh.

Katarina looks at me and then out the window. "What?" she questions.

I glance back through the windshield. That's when I see the end of a rifle pointed at us, and my arm shoots out to push her to the floor of the vehicle. "Stay down." My foot hits the pedal and I take off, just as a bullet hits the back passenger window and glass flies everywhere.

Katarina's scream pierces my fucking heart, long

before it rings out in my ears. Whoever the fuck this is, I'm going to tear them apart, limb by limb.

The barricade opens just before I drive through it. People are running in every direction. "Okay, you're good. Sit up and put your seat belt on." I look at a shaken Katarina on the floor of the car. "Please," I add more softly.

I watch as she slowly climbs back on her seat, and her hands shake as she attempts to plug the metal tongue into the buckle. Grabbing the belt with one hand, I quickly click it into place and adjust it around her shoulder.

"What was that?" she asks.

"That was a dead man fucking walking," I grit out between clenched teeth. My phone rings through the speaker of the car. Tapping the button, I answer. "Pops, what took you so long?" I grunt.

"Luca, what can I do for you?" he asks, clearly agitated.

"Meet me at home. I'm bringing Katarina. We were just fucking shot at on Broadway."

He's silent for a moment. It's how my pops processes things. He thinks, and he's careful with his words. "Where are you now?"

"I'm forty minutes from home."

"Are you being followed?"

"No. We're not. The fucker was in the building across the street from Joe's."

"Okay," he says. "And, Luca, don't do anything reckless. Just get yourself home," he's quick to add.

"Got it." I disconnect the call and look over at Katarina, who is still shaking. "You're going to be okay, bellezza. I'm not going to let anything happen to you." I give her hand a reassuring squeeze.

"I'm sorry I've dragged you into my mess."

"I'm not," I tell her. "This is nothing I can't handle, babe."

"I don't want to be a burden, Luca."

"You are anything but a burden. We're going to my parents' estate. It's the safest place for you right now—that house is locked up like Fort Knox."

"I need to get Amy out of the house, Luca. What if this psycho turns up and she's there?"

"I'll get her out." I hit a button on my phone and call Izzy.

"Lil coz, now's really not a good time," Izzy's voice fills the car.

"Iz, I need you to do something for me. Go to Katarina's place, pick up her assistant, and bring her to my parents' house."

"I happen to know your mother very well, Luca. Which means I know for a fact she taught you Neanderthals manners," my cousin counters with that tone of hers.

"Please," I add through gritted teeth.

"Okay, but why am I picking up your girlfriend's assistant?"

"Because someone just took a fucking shot at us on Broadway, and I'm heading home now. Katarina would like to know that her friend isn't left alone in her house, in case the fucker decides to go there next."

"Please, for the love of God, tell me you didn't get shot again," Izzy says.

"I didn't. But my car did. Fucking idiot. I'm going to take my time torturing him."

"Okay, I'll meet you at your parents' place."

"Oh, and, Izzy, bring pizza," I add, hanging up before she can argue with me.

Chapter Twenty-One

Katarina

I've been around opulence for a few years now. Some of the artists I've become friends with are not shy when it comes to flashing around their wealth. This though, Luca's childhood home, is something else altogether. If you could even call it a home. It's huge, stately, almost what you'd think a president would live in.

However, the moment I walk through the front door, I can see the difference. Because it's not just a big house; it's a home. From the photos that frame the walls of the foyer, down to the vases full of flowers on the hall tables, little trinkets are scattered around various surfaces in a way that makes no design sense at all.

I cling to Luca's hand as he leads me farther inside. I'm trying to take in as much of my surroundings as I can. It's fascinating that this is how he grew up. In a home filled with memories—good memories judging by the smiling faces of the four boys that fill many pictures. He leads me into a library. A freaking library.

"Ma?" Luca calls out as we enter the room.

"Luc, your father said you were stopping by." Mrs. Valentino, or Holly as she insisted I call her, walks around a wall of shelves.

"Yeah, where is he?" Luca asks.

"In his office," she says.

"Great." Luca turns to me. "I'll be right back. Make yourself at home."

My eyes go as wide as saucers. He's leaving me *here*? I want to beg him not to go, not to leave me alone.

"You're safe. I won't be long," Luca whispers into my ear when I don't immediately release his hand. I nod, though I still don't want to let go of him.

"Holly, you in here?" a female voice calls over the threshold of the room.

Luca smiles wide and turns around. "Zia Lola, I didn't know you were in town." He addresses the beautiful woman with long, wavy brown hair as she approaches him. A handsome older man follows behind her.

"James and I were visiting my parents. Thought we'd stop in and see your mom and dad," the woman says.

"Zia Lola, this is my girlfriend, Katarina," Luca introduces me. "Katarina, my Aunt Lola and Uncle James."

"Hello, it's nice to meet you." I don't realize I'm using my 'press voice' until Luca looks at me with his brows furrowed.

"Oh, believe me, it's my pleasure to meet you. I heard what Luca did, but why didn't anyone tell me you two were dating? We actually have someone famous in the family!" Luca's Aunt Lola exclaims excitedly.

"Ah, Zia Lola, I'm a pro football player. Pretty sure I'm famous," Luca pouts.

"Yeah, how many games have you played professionally again?" This comes from yet another beautiful woman, younger, with long blonde hair and a dark complexion.

"Izzy?" Luca questions.

"Well, I'm not Mother Theresa," the woman I now know is *Izzy* says.

"What the fuck did you do to your hair?" Luca asks, horrified.

"I heard blondes have more fun, and I wanted to have fun." She shrugs.

"And did you? Have fun?"

"So much, until you called and pussy blocked me," she says.

"Ew, TMI, Iz. The only thing I wanna know is a name." Luca's face is twisted in disgust.

"Never gonna happen, Luc. Pizza's in the dining room. I'm hungry. Katarina, join me."

"Ah, sure," I say, because I feel like *no* really isn't an option. Especially considering Izzy reaches out and grabs hold of my hand, and I have no choice but to let go of Luca and follow her.

"Izzy, be nice," Luca calls after us.

"I'm always nice. Just ask the guy I left behind with blue balls." She laughs.

"I'll go with them," Holly adds and Lola follows her.

I really hope Luca isn't far behind us, because if I'm expected to find my way out of this house, I've got no chance. It could just be my rattled nerves, but I swear it takes a full five minutes of walking down corridors and through rooms to get to the dining table that's currently stacked with pizza boxes.

"Katy, thank god!" Amy, who was sitting on a chair, jumps up and runs towards me. Her small arms sling around my waist. "I was so freaking worried," she says, her voice quieter.

"I know. I'm sorry," I tell her, returning the gesture and hugging the crap out of her. Without Zane around, Amy has become the closest friend I have. And in the music industry, good friends really are hard to come by. I lucked out when I found my personal assistant. I can't imagine doing any of this without her. She might be on my payroll, but that doesn't make her any less of a friend.

"FYI, Liam is blowing up my phone looking for you," she whispers so everyone else in the room can't hear.

"It's fine. I'll tell him I was creating a new song." I laugh.

Liam is a hard-ass, but that's his job. He's supposed to push me, to keep me going when I want to give up. And he does. He's never gone too far, never tried to take advantage or accepted less-than-stellar contracts that will just fill the kitty. Every move, every deal he makes for Kat Star, is strategic. Each one a rung on the ladder to the top. I do need to call him back. I shouldn't let him think I'm AWOL, just running off doing whatever I want. I mean, it's not like a lot of other artists don't do that. Really, he got the A-plus student with me. I've never been into the party scene, and I don't partake in the whole *sex drugs and rock and roll* bullshit. I sing, and I'm blessed to be able to make a really good living doing what I love.

"Do you have a new song?" Amy asks, not so quietly as she pulls away from me.

"Oh my god, can we hear it?" Lola squeals.

"Ah, it's not really a song yet, just words in my head. But when it's finished, I'll make sure you guys are one of the first to hear it," I tell her. I feel bad when her face drops, but I don't have a song. I have a few lines, no melody, nothing.

"Oh, that's okay." Lola's voice is noticeably lower and her eyes cast to the side. I don't know her, but she seems to be the softer Valentino. Not that the girls I have met in this family aren't lovely, but there's something about Lola that calls to me, and not wanting to disappoint her, I close my eyes and start singing one of my songs.

"They say memories fade,
But my memories, I can't evade.
Broken bones, bruises, hospital trips.
You left me with a razor blade.
You left me there to die.
But all I did was fly.
I won't let you destroy me anymore.
I've had enough of the memories, the
flashbacks, and the tears.
Yeah, those memories, I've shoved them in a
drawer.
The only person who can hurt me is me, and I
won't let that be my fate.
You tried to destroy me, but I've beaten all my
fears."

Opening my eyes when I finish the first chorus, I look around the room. Everyone apart from Amy is looking at me with a very strained expression, but

Lola is the first to speak. "I haven't heard that, but it's beautiful," she says, wiping a stray tear from her eye.

"I'm sorry. I didn't mean to upset you." Damn it, now I feel even worse.

"These are happy tears. I just… you have an amazing voice, Katarina, and those lyrics are just… a lot," Lola says.

"Okay, I don't know about all of you, but I'm eating this pizza before those idiot cousins of mine come in and steal it all." Izzy opens a box and reaches in for a slice.

I'm thankful for her change of direction. "Wait, Luca's not actually an idiot, is he? I mean, I was questioning the whole brains or looks thing with him, because can one person really have it all? It seems unlikely. Right?" I spit out and then look to his mother. "Sorry, Holly, you just breed really beautiful children."

"Don't be sorry. And, no, despite what Izzy will have you believe, Luca is not an idiot," she says. "He chose you, so there must be some sort of intelligence in there," she adds with a laugh.

"If he were smart, he'd learn how to dodge a bullet by now. I swear that kid's like a magnet, just attracting lead everywhere he goes." Izzy shakes her head. And I immediately feel like shit again, knowing full well it's my fault he 'caught' the bullet that was meant for me.

"What's your favorite? Mine's plain cheese." Lola stands next to me, pointing to the box in front of us, and my eyes travel up her arm unintentionally. That's when I see it. The large scar that runs up the length of her wrist. A scar that matches the one on my own arm. Noticing where my gaze has landed, she tugs at her sleeve and tucks her wrist behind her back. I don't want her to think I'm judging her or anything so I do the only thing I can think of.

I lift my arm and turn it to face her. Without words, because none are needed, our eyes connect and it's like we have formed some kind of kindred bond. Which is strange. Lola grabs my hand and guides me to a chair. I pick up a piece of cheese pizza and add it to my plate. Before I know it, we're all sitting around the table and the conversation is back to Izzy's new hair color. The room fills with more women as we all sit, eat pizza, and drink red wine that somehow appeared out of nowhere. I don't remember who brought it in, but I'm thankful they did. I'm sitting next to Amy, with Lilah and Maddie, who both arrived about fifteen minutes ago, on my left. Savannah, Matteo's wife, is sitting opposite us. And then there's Holly, Lola, and Izzy next to them. Romeo's wife is the last to enter and plops herself down in the remaining chair.

"Wine, I need wine." She sighs.

"What's wrong?" Holly asks her.

"I married a fucking Valentino." Livvy sighs. "I'm tired. I think he's trying for baby number two already."

"You can turn him down, you know." Izzy scrunches up her face like she's going to puke.

"Holly, you might want to cover your ears," Livvy says.

"I'm going to get more wine." Mrs. Valentino makes a fast escape from the room, and I'm wondering if I should follow her.

"It's like his dick is coated in cocaine. I'm addicted. I can't get enough of it. Like, seriously, I read the honeymoon stage is supposed to wear off. Does it ever wear off?" Livvy asks, her pointed question directed at her sisters-in-law.

"Not for me, and I hope it never does," Maddie answers.

"Nope, I'm still making up for the years I wasted denying him," Savannah says, and I remember Luca telling me about her being Matteo's best friend since they were kids.

"Argh, I just want to sleep. Just for one whole, solid day without someone wanting to get inside me or someone who came from inside me needing me to keep them alive," Livvy says. "But I also want the orgasms. I really don't think I'm asking for all that much."

"You know, T and I would be more than happy to keep Matilda overnight so you can get some rest," Holly says, walking back into the room with two more bottles of red wine.

"If you can convince Romeo to let her have a

sleepover, then she's all yours. But good luck." Livvy shrugs.

"Mmm, you're forgetting I raised these boys. I know each and every one of their weaknesses." Holly smirks.

Chapter Twenty-Two

Luca

I'm sitting in the auditorium watching Katarina practice for her upcoming concert. I love watching her; it's become my favorite pastime. And listening to her. That voice of hers really is amazing. She's standing front and center on the stage singing to me. Her eyes lock on mine. This woman has a way of making me feel like I'm the only one in the room. Even though we're surrounded by dancers, stagehands, and lighting and sound techs.

I never appreciated how much effort goes into one of these performances, but Katarina has one of the best work ethics I've ever seen. She closes her eyes as she belts out the chorus of one of her songs. Her voice surrounds me. And then, like a beacon, my eyes hone in on it.

That red fucking dot, right in the middle of her chest.

"No!" I scream, jump out of my seat, and run for the stage. "Kat, get down!" I yell out.

She can't hear me. Her eyes are closed and she can't see me. The sound of the gunshot can barely be heard over the music. But I hear it. I fucking hear it. Katarina's eyes open wide, and she looks at me, then down at herself. Her hand covers her chest before she pulls it away and stares at the blood that now covers it. And she drops. I rush onto the stage, falling to my knees next to her.

"Kat, no. Katarina, open your eyes. You're okay. You're going to be okay," I tell her. "Someone call 9-1-1 now!" I scream and look around at everyone going about their business. No one has stopped working. What the fuck are they doing? "Call an ambulance!" I scream again. Cradling her head in my lap, I apply pressure to the hole in her chest. "No, you can't leave me, bellezza. You can't. Please open your eyes, baby, just open them," I cry.

"Luca?"

I hear her voice. Someone's shaking me. That's when my eyes snap open and I'm staring at Katarina's face, staring back down at me. Did I get it wrong? Was I the one who got shot? Again?

"It's just a dream, Luca. We're okay. I'm okay," she says. My arms snatch out and I pull her body onto mine, her head resting on my chest. My heart is still racing from the image of her on the ground, lifeless. "It was just a dream, Luca," she repeats, her hand rubbing small, soothing circles on my bare chest.

"I'm sorry I woke you," I say, my voice hoarse like I've been screaming.

"It's okay."

Rolling to my side, I lie with Katarina in my arms. I can see the sun rising through the sheer curtains on the windows.

"Do you want to talk about it?" Katarina asks.

"I have to get to practice," I tell her, kissing her forehead and untangling myself from her body. I make quick work of getting changed. Picking up my gym bag, I walk back into my bedroom to find Katarina sitting upright in the bed.

"This is the fifth night in a row, Luca. One of these days you're going to have to talk about it," she says, referring to the recurring fucking nightmare I keep having.

"I'm fine. I gotta go. I'll see you later." I bend over and kiss her gently on the lips. It's on the tip of my tongue to tell her I love her. But that's crazy. We've only been dating for three weeks now. But those three words fucking haunt me. What if I never get to tell her? What if we don't have the time?

I can't tell her like this, when I'm rushing out the door. So I don't. I turn and walk out, avoiding any and all emotional crap I'm not ready to face or deal with.

"YO, Valentino, how's the hole healing up?" Clayton, a wide receiver, asks the minute I walk into the locker room for practice.

"Slowly," I grunt, throwing my bag onto a wooden bench in front of my locker.

I've been instructed by the team doctors not to work out. Not to do any kind of physical activity. What the fuck would they know about healing from a bullet wound anyway? I know my body *and* its limitations. There is no way I'm going months without working out. It's been three weeks now and I'm antsy as fuck. I need to get back out on that field. I need to do something to take my mind off of the fact that I haven't fucking caught this motherfucker who's out for Katarina's blood.

My hands clench into fists at my side. The noise in here from all my teammates talking shit should be enough to drown out my thoughts. It's not. I dig for my phone and message Katarina. I don't like how I left her this morning. I start typing out an apology and then delete it.

Valentinos don't apologize. We're never wrong.

It's something Theo has drilled into me since we

were kids. Which, now that I think about it, is fucking ridiculous. I was wrong. I was an ass. And for that, I am fucking sorry. I just don't know how to tell her as much. I try again.

ME:

Let me know when you're up. XX

It's not Shakespeare, but I'm not fucking Romeo. My twin could write a sonnet if he wanted to. He's the one who got the brains out of the two of us—a kid genius, that one. My brother could have skipped years ahead of school, but he refused to leave me, choosing to stay by my side instead.

I change into some workout clothes, tie up my shoes, and head out to the field. It fucking sucks sitting here on the bench and not being out there with my teammates.

"How long did they say you'd be out for?" Jonah, a running back, plops down next to me with a cast around his ankle that wasn't there yesterday.

"Too fucking long. You?" I ask him, nodding to his leg.

"Same, man." He sighs.

"What happened?"

"You wouldn't believe it if I told you," he says

"You'd be surprised what I'd believe."

"I was with this chick…"

As soon as he says the word chick, I tune out. I've heard Jonah's stories before, and he's one sick fuck. And that's saying a lot coming from me.

"Told you, you wouldn't believe it," he finishes and nudges my shoulder.

"Only you, Jonah." I smirk at him, pretending I was fully engaged in the conversation. I have no idea what he actually did to his foot. Nor do I really care.

"There's a party tonight. You gonna come?"

"Can't. Got shit to do," I grunt out.

"You need to learn how to unwind. We've never even had a beer together," he says.

"I don't drink. One kidney, remember?" I remind him.

"I don't know how you do it." He shakes his head.

"It's not as hard as you think," I say, pushing to my feet. I can't just sit on this bench for the next few hours. I start walking the field, wishing like anything that I could just fucking run.

I WALK into the house and am immediately met by a sound that always tears at my heart. Matilda's cry. I hate it. That baby girl should never cry. Picking up my pace, I find Livvy in the living room with Katarina and Matilda—the latter is still screaming her lungs out.

"What the fuck did you do to her?" I ask, dropping my bag on the floor and reaching for my niece.

"Nothing. She's cutting teeth, Luca. Babies do that," Livvy says, handing Matilda right over to me before I have the chance to ask. "If you think you can do better, go for it."

I cradle Matilda to my chest, rubbing small circles on her back. Leaning down next to her ear, I whisper, "Per favore non piangere, bella." *Please don't cry, beautiful.* Matilda starts to settle, and her whimpers turn into hiccupping sobs. "Shhh, Zio Luca is here. It's okay, Tilly. I've got you," I tell her. Livvy appears irritated as she watches me soothe Matilda, while Katarina has a look of awe. "What?" I ask both of them.

"I suck at motherhood." Livvy sighs, leaning back into the sofa.

"You don't suck at anything, Liv," I tell her, believing every word. I think my sister-in-law might be the one person I know who's smarter than Romeo.

"Argh, then why does she settle so quickly for you?" she says.

"What can I say? I have the touch." I shrug. "Where's Romeo?" I ask, knowing he has to be around here somewhere. He's never too far away from his wife and daughter.

"He went to get food. Half an hour ago." Liv gives me a pointed glare. There's something she's not saying. Something she doesn't want to mention in front of Katarina. As much as my family has accepted her into our world, they're cautious. We can never be too careful when it comes to the inner workings of the family. As much as I trust Katarina, I've avoided telling her anything too personal. Mostly for her own safety.

Leaning down, I kiss Katarina softly on her lips. "Hi." I smile at her.

"Hi."

I straighten up. "I'll be back." I walk out of the room and head down a hall. I need to call Romeo and find out what the fuck he's doing. Passing Danny and John in the foyer, I give them a nod. "Anything I need to know?" I ask them. I had both of them on Katarina watch while I've been at training.

"All quiet, Luc," they reply.

"That's good." I continue down the hall to the office. It's not a room I use often, but right now I want a secluded place to make a call. Tilly's hiccups have died down. Kissing the top of her head, I take a seat and dig my phone out of my pocket. Just as I'm about to dial Romeo, I hear someone in the adjoining bathroom. There shouldn't be anyone in here. Standing, I stick my head out the door and nod to John. When he reaches me, I pass him Matilda. "Take her back to Livvy and stay with them," I tell him.

He peers into the empty office before turning and walking back down the hall with Matilda. Opening the desk drawer, I take out the pistol that's stored there. My steps are quiet as I approach the bathroom. Turning the handle, I have my gun aimed and ready as I push the door open.

"What the fuck?" I hiss out, lowering my weapon when I find Izzy on the floor huddled over the toilet.

"Close the door," she tells me.

I do as she says but stay in the bathroom. "What's wrong?" I ask her, squatting down to her level.

"Nothing. People get sick all the time, Luca. It's perfectly normal," she sasses back.

I tilt my head and look her up and down. "For the sake of this city, I really fucking hope it's food poisoning and not morning sickness." Her whole face pales at my words. "Fuck, Iz, what have you done?" For the first time in my life, I see tears fall from her eyes as I lower myself to the floor and hug her to my chest. "It's okay. Whatever it is, we'll fix it," I tell her.

"I don't think we can fix this, Luc. I really fucked up this time."

"We're Valentinos. We can fix anything," I remind her.

"Right. You're right. I'm being ridiculous." Izzy pulls out of my arms and stands. "I just ate something wrong. That's all," she says, turning the faucet on.

I don't for one second believe her, but if she's not ready to face whatever it is she's going through, then I'm not going to force her. Yet. I'll leave it for now, but this is a conversation we will be revisiting.

Chapter Twenty-Three

Katarina

I scribble the lyrics on the paper. The words are flowing out of me faster than anything before. I guess it's true what they say about artists and their muses, because Luca seems to be mine. I'm not sure if I'll ever record this song, or if it's just something I need to get out onto paper, something I need to put to a melody. I never imagined that while I'm terrified of the attempts on my life, I'm also living my best moments right now.

When I'm with Luca, I can pretend that I'm normal. Well, almost normal. I can be myself. He doesn't expect me to be the pop star. He never wants anything from me. Well, anything other than my body, which is something I'll happily hand to him on a silver platter.

I thought I'd had good sex before. I was wrong. The things Luca does to my body, the pleasure he wrings from me, is unlike anything I've ever felt. It's addictive. I honestly can't get enough of it.

I'm humming out the tune to the lyrics now scrawled across paper. This whole song is about the whirlwind relationship I'm experiencing right now. I've often drawn inspiration from my own life, my own trials and tribulations. Honestly, it's refreshing to have it come from a place of love this time.

Love. Is that what Luca and I have? I'm not sure. The only relationship I've seen that represents the truest form of love is Zane and Marcia. I guess I can add a lot more names to the list now that I've met the Valentino family. Luca's parents seem happy, devoted to each other and their children. Then there's all of his brothers. They're happily married. I haven't known them long, so I'm taking it at face value from what I've observed.

I want that. I want that undying devotion from a partner, someone to go through life with me. I want a family of my own, which is new for me. I never thought I could have any of those things until a few weeks ago. It's insane how much I want it now. After being with Luca, I don't just *want* that semblance of a normal, happy life. I'm craving it.

Can I have both though? My career, all the success, *and* a family? That's the million-dollar question.

The door to the studio opens. I look up and try not to show my disappointment when I see my manager and not Luca. I know Liam's been trying to pin me down to finalize the details for the tour that I'm scheduled to go on next month. Truthfully, I've been avoiding it. And him. I know I have to do it. I'm contractually obligated with the label. And I want to go. I love being on stage. I love the crowd, and I love singing. What I'm avoiding is the thought of leaving Luca behind. Of coming back to find he's moved on and found someone else in my absence. A man like him won't be lonely for long. I'm certain all he'd have to do is walk into a club and summon a woman over, and she'd willingly be his for how ever long he wanted her.

Have I tortured myself with thoughts of Luca refusing to wait for me? Yes, far more than I care to admit. Sometimes I just find it hard to get out of my own head.

"Don't be so happy to see me, Kat." Liam sits opposite me, crossing his legs and hunching over to get my attention.

I'm on the floor, my back up against the wall, with my guitar next to me and my writing pad on my lap. "I'm always happy to see you, Liam."

"Mmhmm, well, I'm glad I finally caught you. We need to finalize some things for the Homegrown Tour." He pulls out a stack of manila folders from his briefcase and starts spreading the various papers and photos in front of me.

"Can't you just pick for me?" I pout.

"Nope, this is all you. Have you gone over the final dress fittings and hair and makeup with Hailey?" he asks.

"Not yet. She's been absent a lot lately. I guess I haven't been going to as many public events so I just haven't seen her." I'm sure that's why she's been quiet. Though, now that I think about it, I'm not certain that explains it either, seeing as she'll usually message me about the latest trends and styles regardless of what my calendar looks like.

Am I that caught up in Luca that I'm neglecting everyone else in my life? I don't think I've been. I've made sure to check in with Amy every day, Liam at least three times a week. I'm still making my scheduled workout appointments, much to Luca's annoyance. He insists that he can give me a better workout than any private instructor. I'm sure he could, but how can I focus on exercise when I have him to look at?

"Make sure you get those details finalized. Your appearance on stage is everything. I'm sure I don't have to tell you that," Liam says.

"I thought it was my voice."

"Well, that too. Is that a new song?" He nods at

the notepad with a bunch of jumbled words scribbled across it.

"It's a work in progress."

We spend the next thirty minutes going over some of the finer details of the tour. And when Liam finally leaves, I return to the task at hand. I think I might already have the lyrics part of the song done.

Reckless Love
I'm not afraid of what's hunting me
My thunder roars, lightning cracks, but I won't flee.
The storm brings out a wild love in me,
A reckless faith on an uncharted sea.
[Chorus]
'Cuz your reckless love never fails me.
Your recklessness carries me away
Oh, your reckless love sets me free.
[Verse 2]
I've been feeling down in a broken, stormy night.
I've searched for peace, but never found the light.
But then you came, darkness and light in one.
Oh, your recklessness won
[Chorus]

'Cuz your reckless love never fails me.
Your recklessness carries me away.
Oh, your reckless love sets me free.
[Bridge]
No fear can overcome this kind of love.
There's nothing holding me back.
This is my moment to shine.
I'm going to take back my life. It's time.
[Chorus]
'Cuz your reckless love never fails me.
Your recklessness carries me away.
Oh, your reckless love sets me free.

My hand comes up and wipes at the tear that rolls down my cheek. These words are my soul. They're so deep, so personal, that I'm not sure I can ever really share them with anyone else. When I put a song out into the world, it's no longer mine. It becomes theirs, my fans. They own it. They create memories to it. Get married, have their first kiss. It's a powerful notion that my words can bring people so much. I've had a ton of fan mail proclaiming how my words spoke to them, changed their lives for the better. Maybe these lyrics could encourage others to go out and find their love, and not to settle for anything less than what they deserve.

My mother's image pops into my mind, a rare

moment when I don't remember her with black eyes or covered in cuts and bruises. This memory is of her beautiful face, her huge smile as she spins me around in the park. The sun shining down on us. Then he's there, standing off in the distance and yelling at her to hurry up. My father.

Shaking my head, I clear the thoughts away. I've never really been able to recall happy moments with my mom without my dad barreling through them.

Walking out of the studio, I make my way into the kitchen, passing Danny—one of the many men Luca has stationed around me at all times. They're nice, always super polite, and although they look like people I wouldn't want to mess with, they've never made me feel anything but safe.

"Danny, you hungry? I'm going to make dinner." I smile at him.

"Ma'am, I believe Mrs. Donatello sent some food over earlier. It's in your fridge. As much as I'd love to have some, I fear Mr. Valentino is likely to shoot me if I do."

"Okaaaay. I don't think he's actually gonna shoot you, but it's your loss if you're too chicken." I laugh.

"When it comes to those Valentino boys, they won't let anyone touch their nonna's cooking. They're heathens, ma'am." There's a slight smile on his face, very slight. If you weren't looking, you'd miss it for sure.

I continue to make my way to the kitchen, curious to see what Luca's grandmother sent over. I haven't met his grandparents yet. He talks about a bunch of extended family in Australia as well—though I have heard him on the phone to his cousins there, Hope and Lily, another set of twins. His mom is also a twin I've learned. Which is weird. Is it normal for twins to have twins? I hope it's not something that runs in the family, because I really don't want to have two babies growing inside me at once.

I pause. My legs freezing on the spot. What the freaking hell was that? I am *not* thinking about having babies with Luca. Except, now that the image is in my head, I know it's stuck there. Seeing how good he is with his nephews and nieces, I know he'd be a great father. I feel it down to my soul. How could he not be? He had the perfect parents to learn from, leaving me to wonder what kind of mother I'd be...

Chapter Twenty-Four

Luca

I'm lying awake with Katarina's head on my chest. She's asleep as my fingers idly twirl through the ends of her hair. How does she get it so fucking soft?

My mind won't shut off, constantly going over what I missed. Why we haven't been able to find the fucker who's after my girl. There haven't been any more attempts on her life. Although that probably has a lot to do with me keeping her indoors. If we're not at my house, we're at hers. If I'm not at training or out combing the streets looking for this fucking cockroach, then I'm with her. And when I can't be with her, I make sure my most trusted men are. It's funny how much my life has changed in the last few weeks. It's fast, but then again, I've always done everything fast. Grabbed life by the balls and taken charge.

Why should a relationship be any different?

I didn't know what I was missing. That's a lie. I've always envied Romeo's relationship with Livvy. Not because I like my sister-in-law like that. I don't. Never have. It's because of their connection, they're undying commitment to each other. I have that with my family, sure, but it's a different kind of commitment. What I feel for Katarina is fierce, primal. I want to keep her out of harm's way, which technically would be keeping her out of my way too, because my life is anything but safe. I can't see myself letting her go. Ever. So I have to work double hard to make sure she's always got security, always protected to the fullest extent of my abilities.

My wounds are healing. The docs still won't let me back on the field yet, which I think is a crock of fucking shit. I can throw a football now just as well as I could before.

My phone vibrates on the bedside table, and my arm snaps out and picks it up so it doesn't disturb Katarina. The time reads one thirty a.m. It's never a good thing when my phone rings this early—or is it late?

"Yeah?" I answer as quietly as I can. I shuffle out from underneath Katarina. She stirs but quickly settles down again. So I creep out of the room with my phone to my ear.

"You got mail," Romeo says.

"What?" I ask, not trusting my ears. It's what I've been waiting to hear. We've got him.

"The parcel turned up at the wrong address, but it's for you. It was delivered to a basement in Hell's Kitchen—of all fucking places," he says. My brother is speaking in code, in case we're ever bugged by the Feds. What he really means is that he's found the guy, the one who's tried to kill Katarina… twice.

"Where are you?"

"Warehouse four."

"I'll be right there. Don't open it without me," I say and cut the call. I walk through the house, and it's not until I get to the door that I remember I sent my men home earlier tonight.

Fuck. I dial Izzy's number. "Luca? Are you shot?" she asks.

I roll my eyes. It seems to be a running joke with my family now. I've been shot *twice*. It's not a frequent fucking occurrence. "No, I need you to come to Katarina's," I tell her.

"Why?"

"Because I have to run an errand. I can't leave her alone."

"You do know I'm not a babysitter, right?"

"Izzy, please, there are very few people I trust, and you are lucky enough to make that list."

"Fine, I'll be there, but you owe me."

"Thank you." I hang up, and as I go to pocket my phone, my body moving on autopilot, I look down and realize I'm only wearing a pair of black briefs. So I make my way back to the bedroom, pick up my jeans, shirt, and shoes from the floor and exit with one last look at Katarina. She's curled up in the blankets.

Fuck, she's breathtakingly beautiful.

I go into the foyer to wait for Izzy and get dressed. As soon as I see her vehicle pull up to the gate, I run out the door. By the time she stops in front of the house, I'm at the driver's side of my car. "Thanks, Iz. She's asleep. I'll be back before she's awake."

"No worries." Izzy waves as she walks up to the front door of the house.

———

AN HOUR LATER, I'm pulling into a lot full of cars I recognize. Looks like this is going to be a family affair. Stretching my arms, I crack my knuckles and shake out my hands as I walk into the dimly lit warehouse. I haven't been here in a while, probably around two years. However, the moment I step inside, it feels like just yesterday.

I'm eager to rid the earth of this fucker. To eradicate any threat to Katarina. I want to be able to move on from this, to see her shine in her element, up on that stage without the constant worry of a bullet ending up in her chest. The nightmares I've been having don't just haunt my sleep. They fucking stay with me constantly, the fear ever present in the back of my mind.

It's time to end it.

"Why am I always the last one to the party?" I complain as my eyes land on each one of my brothers, my father, and my Uncle Neo.

"You drive the slowest," Matteo says with a shrug.

"Fuck off," I grunt. My gaze hones in on the fucker currently hanging from a butcher's hook, rusty chains wrapped around his waist. "So, you're the cocksucker who thinks he can take something that belongs to me?" I ask, my steps measured as I approach him.

My pops is sitting on a chair at the side of the room. Uncle Neo stands next to him with his back resting on the brick wall. They appear almost bored. Then again, no one told them they *had* to be here. It was their choice.

"I don't know what you're talking about," the bastard insists.

"What's your name?" I ask him. I already know it. I just want him to give it up.

"Jack," he spits out.

"Jack? Are you sure about that?"

"What's it fucking matter? Whoever you're looking for, I'm not him."

"My sources say otherwise." I glance to my left,

where my three brothers stand. "You did tell me this was him, right? Aaron Madsen?" I ask them.

"It's him." Theo nods.

"Thank fuck, I'd hate to kill the wrong guy."

"What? No, it's not me!" the guy screams, thrashing about, which only causes the chains to cut into the skin on his wrists more. Blood drips down both of his arms.

"You know, they all say that. It's never fucking true though, is it, Aaron?" I walk around him, circling him like the prey he is. "I'm feeling merciful today, Aaron, so it might just be your lucky day." The lie slips from my tongue like melting butter. "Tell me who put you up to it. Tell me why you have a boner for killing Kat Star," I say, stopping directly in front of him.

His eyes widen. He finally understands why he's here. "I... I... didn't." He shakes his head.

"You did. I saw you. You shot me. But you already know that, don't you?" I ask him.

"No, you don't understand. We're in love. I love her. I'm saving her. We're going to be together," he says it like he fucking believes the next-level crazy coming out of his mouth.

"You don't kill people you love," I tell him.

The fucker shakes his head again. "She has to die to be saved. He hurt her. She's damaged here."

"Who hurt her?" I ask him.

"Her father, he hurt her. She needs to be saved," he says the words over and over again.

"How do you know what her father did to her? How do you know Kat Star?" I question him.

"We grew up together. I told you we're in love. I'm helping her." The scary thing is he actually believes every fucking word spewing from his mouth.

"Untie him. Bring him to the top," I direct Matteo.

"Why? What's at the top?" Aaron screams.

"Your freedom." I smile at him and walk out, followed by my pops and Uncle Neo as I head to the roof. The building's only three stories, but it's high enough for what I want to do.

"Luca, it's three in the morning. Think you can hurry this up a bit?" Pops says from behind me.

"It won't take much longer. You think I wanted to drag my ass out of bed?" I grunt back at him. "You know you don't have to stay. I get it. Old age catches up to everyone, Pops." I laugh, jogging up the stairs a tad faster so he can't reach the back of my head.

Number one rule in the family: Never underestimate the boss.

Before I can reach the top landing, my father is behind me, delivering me that slap to the back of the head I knew was coming. "I'm more than happy to show you what this old man is still capable of, smartass," he says.

"I would offer to go into the ring with you, but I don't want to upset Ma when I send you home bleeding." I laugh again.

"Fucking little smartass," my father seethes between clenched teeth.

"You know who you remind me of, Luca?" This comes from my Uncle Neo.

"Who?" I ask.

"No one, because I've never met anyone that fucking stupid." He smirks.

I blink at him, giving him my well-practiced blank expression. "Huh, I must be too stupid to understand the hidden meaning there. You might have to break it down for me."

Just as his mouth drops to speak again, the door to the roof opens and Matteo and Theo are dragging a kicking and screaming Aaron through it. Romeo is behind them. His eyes catch mine.

You good? His silent question is directed right at me as our eyes meet.

Yep. I give him a slight nod. I don't remember a time we haven't been able to read each other, to have conversations without the need for words. Ma says it's a twin thing.

I walk up to Aaron, and my right arm swings out, connecting with the side of his head. His eyes roll back before his body goes limp. Matteo and Theo release him, letting his body fall to the ground. I reach for a piece of rope and tie his legs together, attaching the free end to a cement pillar.

"I'm going to need a can of gasoline," I tell Romeo, who nods his head before running back through the door to get the accelerant. "Help me throw him over," I ask my older brother as I grab Aaron's legs, and Theo picks up the top half of the fucker's body.

Walking to the edge of the building, we toss him over the railing. As the fucker hangs there, Romeo returns with the can.

"What's the plan here, Luca?" Uncle Neo questions me.

I smile. "I'm going to wait for the son of a bitch to come to, and then you'll see."

He's not waking up in a hurry. I know he's not dead, just out cold from the direct blow to his skull. Picking up the can of gasoline, I tip a bit over the railing and on to his face. That does it. He stirs before taking in the fact that he's now hanging upside down from the top of the building.

"What? Help!" he screams, like that shit actually does anything.

I continue to pour the bottle of gasoline on him until it's empty. Throwing the canister to the floor, I hold out a hand to Theo. "Lighter," I say, and wait for him to dig it out of his pocket and place it on my palm. "Thanks."

"Are you fucking crazy? Let me up! Help! Someone, help!" Aaron yells out.

"I'll let you up when you tell me how you knew we'd be at that pizza shop?"

"I-I bugged her studio. I just wanted to hear her sing. I swear," he screams. "Now let me up! Help me!"

"I *am* helping you, Aaron. I'm saving you, really." I shrug my shoulders. "This is your peace," I say as I light the rope that's now soaked in gasoline, watching the fire running a trail all the way down until the flames engulf his body.

Aaron screams, his skin alight as he thrashes around. Moments later, the rope burns through and he falls, his cries silenced by the thud of his body meeting concrete.

"Well, that's one way to do it," Pops says, peeking over the railing. "Though a bullet would have been a hell of a lot quicker and less dramatic."

"Where's the fun in that?" I counter.

Pops shakes his head, with a small smile on his face. "I fucking raised a bunch of heathens," he says to my uncle.

"You did. But it's okay, because I raised a fucking princess," Uncle Neo says proudly—to which every single one of us, except him, bursts out laughing. "What? I dare any one of you fuckers to say Izzy is anything less than fucking perfect." He aims a finger at us, one by one.

And our combined laughter is effectively silenced. I might be fucking reckless, but I don't have an actual death wish. I keep my mouth shut, and so do my brothers.

Pops, though... that man is one crazy bastard. "She's scarier than her fucking mother, and that's saying something, because Angelica is fucking insane," he says. Our Aunt Angelica is his half-sister.

"I hear it runs in the blood." Uncle Neo fires back as we all exit the building. However, as we turn the corner, ready to collect and dispose of the body, we freeze.

"What the fuck?" I ask, my eyes flicking from side to side before landing on the empty scorch mark on the ground. There's no way that fucker survived the fall *and* got up and ran away, especially with all the flesh melted off his body. "How does a dead man disappear on his own?"

"He doesn't. Someone fucking interfered with business that's not theirs. I want you all to gather the family. Meet me back home within the hour," my father says.

"Pops, ever have something like this happen before?" I ask him. Because I sure as fuck haven't.

"Never." He shakes his head.

Chapter Twenty-Five

Katarina

The bed dips next to me and consciousness slowly creeps in as I blink my eyes open. A smile spreads across my lips at the sight that greets me. Luca. Not just Luca, a shirtless Luca with water running down his bare chest. My eyes follow the path of one droplet until it touches the top of the towel he has wrapped around his waist. My lips turn down.

"*That* is ruining my view." I pout with a finger pointed at the plush material.

Luca laughs, but it sounds forced. My eyes travel back up to his. I've seen many of his expressions over the past few weeks. I've seen him angry, happy, upset, frustrated, exhausted... and my favorite, blissed out post-orgasm. But the expression he wears now is not any of those. It's like a dark cloud is hanging over his head. Almost as if the weight of the world is on his shoulders.

"I know you're going to tell me that everything is fine, so before I ask you what's wrong, just know that I already know that everything is *not* fine." I sit upright so we're face to face. "Luca, what's wrong?"

"We have to go to my parents' house for a bit, and I need you to pack a bag," he says.

"Why?"

"It's just safer there." He pushes to his feet. That's *not* it. There's something he's not telling me.

"You know I have enough people in my life feeding me bullshit, so unless you're going to be honest with me, you can just take yourself to your parents' house and I'll stay here," I tell him, and pull the covers up to my chin. As much as I may sound confident and careless, I really don't want him to go without me.

Luca's face hardens. "I'm not leaving you here. Come on, Katarina, just... please pack a bag."

I stare at him as he starts pacing the length of the

bedroom. "Whatever it is, it can't be that bad. Just tell me."

He stops midstride and spins to look at me. Then, without saying a word, he walks to a tanned leather overnight bag that sits on a chair in the corner—a bag that wasn't there last night. Luca pulls out a metal box, places it on the bed, and sits himself across from me. He presses a button on the device before glancing up again.

"What is that?" I ask.

"A scrambler. It interferes with any listening or recording devices that could be in this room," he says.

"Why do you think you need that? Oh my god! Do you think I'm recording you?" I cross my arms over my chest at the accusation.

"No. You, I trust. It's everyone else I don't. What I'm going to tell you, Katarina…" Luca pauses and runs a hand through his hair. "I'm in this, you and me. It's the real deal. This isn't a fling for me, Katarina."

"Okay, this isn't a fling for me either." I have no idea where he's going with this.

"I need to know that you won't want to leave me. That after I tell you this, no matter how much you might hate or despise me, that you won't leave. I need you to know that I would never hurt you, and that you have absolutely no reason to be scared of me."

"Luca, you're scaring me now. Just tell me," I say. I don't think there is anything that would make me leave him.

"Aaron Madsen, do you know the name?" he asks.

My brain works double time, trying to search my memories for any sort of recognition. "The only Aaron I've ever known was a neighbor when I was thirteen. Why?"

"He was the motherfucker sending you all that shit. He was the one trying to kill you, Katarina." Luca takes hold of my hands.

"What? Why would he do that?" My brows furrow. "I was always nice to him. I never bullied him like the other kids. Why would he come after me?"

"He wasn't right in the head. He had fantasies of the two of you living out some love affair in the after-life." Luca's teeth ground together.

"That's insane," I murmur. And then it clicks. "Wait... what do you mean *was*? Why did you say he *was* insane?"

"I killed him," Luca whispers, so low I barely hear him. But I do.

"You killed him? Why?" I ask.

"I will never let anyone who wants to bring any kind of harm to you continue to walk this earth," he says, and I'm not sure how to respond.

Is that what he was worried about? Why he thought I'd leave him? I should be more concerned. Logically, I know that. But logic has absolutely nothing to do with what I feel for this man.

"That's not all. The body's missing," Luca says.

"What do you mean?"

"I'm not going to tell you the details, and not

because I don't trust you, but because I don't want you implicated in my fucked-up world any more than you already are. We were going to get rid of it, but it wasn't there. Someone took him, took *it*."

I shake my head. I don't understand. What does this mean for him? "What? How? I don't get it. Who would take his body, Luca? Where were you? We should look again," I tell him. While I don't know anything about murdering people, what I do know is that a body leaves evidence and evidence leads to questions. Questions that could end up pointing a finger at Luca, who is currently looking at me like I've grown two heads. Perhaps I have, because I just offered to go and help him search for the body of my former next-door neighbor. A man he killed.

"There is no way in hell I'd ever let you help me with any of this. I might be damned already, babe, but you aren't. I will not tarnish your soul with my world."

"You are my world, Luca. If you need help, then I'm going to help in any way I can. Just as I would expect you to do for me."

"Well, me helping you is a given, babe. Have you forgotten the part where I took a bullet for you, literally?" The smirk on his face melts me in all the wrong places. This was a serious conversation. He just told me he killed a guy for me. I shouldn't be feeling the dampness between my now-clenched thighs. "If you really want to help me, you can pack a bag and come to my parents' house," he reminds me.

"How long will we be there? Because I have a tour coming up, and I have rehearsals booked for Friday, Monday, and Tuesday. I can't miss these things."

"You won't. I promise I will get you to every rehearsal. Besides, you really think I'm going to miss the opportunity to see you up on a stage?"

"Rehearsals are not glamourous, far from it," I tell him as I slide off the bed.

"Bellezza, you'd make a cardboard box glamorous."

"Mmm, remember that, on the off chance I lose my voice and end up poor again." I laugh.

I'm not worried about that happening. I've had Liam set up investments with my money. I should be able to retire now and never have to work another day in my life. I sing because, well, honestly, it doesn't feel like work to me. It makes me happy. Almost as happy as doing the man currently sitting on my bed in nothing but a towel. I wonder if we have time for me to find a little... *happiness* before we have to leave.

I walk into my closet and pull down an overnight bag. I'm going to pack the basics and then jump on that man. That's the plan anyway.

"Pops is blowing up my phone. We were supposed to be home an hour ago," Luca calls out.

Well, there goes my plan, I guess.

I throw on a sundress and shove some clothes into my bag. Walking back out, I slip my feet into a pair of slides. "Just so you know, I was planning on spending the morning in bed. With you. And me. Naked. Multiple orgasms were to be had."

"Fuck, bellezza, maybe I can blow off the family a bit longer." Right as he says this, his phone starts ringing.

"Guess not. Come on, before they send a search party after you."

Chapter Twenty-Six

Luca

Holding Katarina's hand, I lead her upstairs. Why am I fucking nervous? Probably because I've never brought a girl into my room at my parents' house. When Romeo and I were teenagers, Theo gave us an apartment in the city. That's where we'd take our girls. Never here.

Opening the door to the bedroom I grew up in, I hold it ajar as Katarina walks past me to enter the room. I close the door behind us and turn on the lights. The curtains are drawn, making it appear darker than it is. I watch silently as Katarina takes it all in, and I try to see it through her eyes. There's a large, king size bed in the center of the room made up in navy bedding. The walls are covered in a mixture of football players and models. The sports posters can stay but the girls need to go, especially considering I've fucked some of them. The reality wasn't anywhere near as good as the fantasy.

"This is where you grew up? This is insane, Luca," Katarina says, spinning around in a circle. "Your bedroom has its own living room." She points out the sitting area with matching two-seater black leather sofas with the black and white solid marble coffee table between them. My PlayStation remote is placed on top.

"It's not that special," I say.

"Luca, I could fit my father's entire trailer in a quarter of this room," Katarina says.

We've spoken a little about her childhood, about her parents. But I haven't wanted to push her to give me more than she's been ready to share. I figure if I'm patient enough, she'll tell me everything in time.

"You know, you're the first girl I've ever brought in here," I admit.

"Are you expecting me to believe you were celibate during your high school years? Because I remember the quarterback at my school. I know I shouldn't stereotype and all. But look at you, Luca, there is no way you didn't have *special friends*," she says, using air quotes around the last two words.

"I had plenty of friends, bellezza. I just never brought them here."

"So, what I'm hearing is... we should christen these sheets," she says, jumping on the bed.

"You're a fucking genius. I swear that's the best fucking idea I've ever heard." I pull the shirt over the back of my head, approaching her like a predator would his prey.

"Mmm, I have lots of good ideas," she tells me.

"Name another one."

"I think you should kiss me." She smirks.

"That *is* a good idea," I say as I climb on top of her, my lips find hers, and my tongue pushes through the seam of her mouth. "Fucking best idea," I mumble into the kiss.

My hand wraps around her throat as I tilt her head back, allowing me better access to devour her mouth. I let myself get lost in her taste, the feel of her soft curves underneath me. Her legs circle my waist, pulling my hips down onto her. Katarina grinds up, pressing her core against the hardness of my cock. Fuck... I reach down and undo the button on my jeans. Sliding the zipper down, I free my cock, giving it a long, hard tug.

"Luca, Pops wants us." Romeo's voice comes from the hallway, loud and clear, followed by the sound of his fist banging on the door.

"Got it," I yell back before turning to Katarina

with a grunt, "Fucking cockblock. Rain check, babe? Make yourself at home. I'm sure you'll find Ma around somewhere if you want to go talk to her. And Maddie, Livvy, and Lilah are here too." I lean down, giving her a quick peck before begrudgingly sliding off the bed and picking up my shirt.

AN HOUR, that's how long I've been sitting in my father's office with my mind constantly drifting to the image of Katarina sprawled out on my bed. I check my phone for the millionth time. She hasn't messaged me. I'm taking that as a sign that she's okay.

I know that this house is on lockdown. No one is getting in or out right now. I didn't tell her that part. I'm hoping she's not going to try to leave. The thing about lockdown, once you know you can't leave, all you want to do is get the fuck out.

"I don't think it's another organization. It was sloppy. They were sloppy. Two people, looks like one woman, one man," Theo says, pointing to a grainy image that was pulled from the camera system on Romeo's Tesla. The warehouse purposely does not have CCTV. No one wants the shit that goes down at that place recorded. It just so happened my twin parked his car facing the side of the building where Aaron… fell.

"Who the fuck are they and what the fuck are they playing at?" I ask.

"That, we don't know yet. We don't have a clear enough image to run facial rec. We're hunting down the car, but it's like finding a needle in a fucking haystack, Luca. There's no fucking plates. They could be anywhere."

"Someone knew we were there. Who?" Romeo presses.

"I didn't even tell my wife," Uncle Neo says.

"I didn't say a word," I add. One by one, everyone else confirms the same.

"Well, there's nothing we can do about it now but go about our lives. I'm sure whoever took that body wants something, and we'll be the first to know what that is," Pops says.

I push to my feet, keen to get back to Katarina. "Great, we can all sit around and twiddle our thumbs while someone plays with the body of the man I killed," I grunt, walking out of the room and down the hallway. I stop outside Romeo's bedroom door—his is right next to mine—and immediately recognized the pair of raised voices coming from inside.

"You can't do this, Iz. It's insane and wrong," Livvy says.

"It's not wrong, and I can do it. Watch me."

I swing the door open. "You might want to talk louder, girls. The neighbors can't quite hear you," I tell them.

"Guess the sausage fest downstairs is finished then?" Izzy rolls her eyes.

"Yep. What's going on? What do you plan on doing that you shouldn't be doing?" I ask her.

"Nothing that concerns you, baby cousin." Izzy stands and attempts to walk around me.

"Whatever you're thinking, don't do it," I tell her. I have no idea what's going on, but if Livvy says it's not right, then chances are it's not fucking right.

"I heard you have more pressing matters to concern yourself with than what I am or am not doing, Luca." Izzy shoves her way past me, making a hasty escape down the hall.

"You good?" I ask Livvy.

"Yep, you?" she replies.

"Been better. Where's my princess?" I ask, scanning the room for Matilda.

"Your mom took her to the pool," she says, picking up her ever attached Kindle and sitting on the black sofa that's a mirror image to the pair I have in my room.

"Cool. I'll leave you to it."

Walking into my own room, I'm assaulted by the scent that is Katarina. Sweet florals mixed with vanilla. Except she's not in here. I peek into the bathroom and find it empty as well. Fuck, I was really hoping to pick up where we left off. I glance at my bed longingly before I turn on my heel, determined to hunt her down and bring her back up here.

Chapter Twenty-Seven

Katarina

Honestly, roaming through Luca's bedroom, getting a glimpse into how he grew up, really highlights the differences between us. His space is like a time capsule from his teenage years. There are shelves lined with football trophies and photos from his high school team. When I was in high school, I never would have dreamed of dating the quarterback. Or anyone on the football team for that matter. I was never part of the popular crowd. I was trailer park trash. Zane, a few other kids from the park, and I would usually hang out under the bleachers. As out of sight as we possibly could be.

Because out of sight was out of mind. Until my dad died. I never went back to school after that. I couldn't risk being shoved into a foster home. I'd heard the stories from some girls I knew who went into the system, and I was determined to not let that shit happen to me. With Zane's help, I managed to survive the two years it took me to turn eighteen. The week of my birthday, he gave me an envelope of cash, a key to a one-bedroom apartment in Brooklyn, and a one-way bus ticket to New York City.

There's a knock at the door, and suddenly I feel like I'm somewhere I shouldn't be. I don't know what I'm supposed to do. Do I answer it? Or hide like the intruder I feel I am?

Hoping option number one is the right choice, I walk to the door and swing it open, faking a confidence I don't feel. Holly stands on the other side with a welcoming smile that instantly puts me at ease.

"We're all heading down to the pool house. I'd love it if you joined us," she says.

"Uh, I didn't bring a suit," I tell her.

"Here. I thought you might need this." Holly holds out a folded blue-and-white striped towel with a two-piece black bikini neatly folded on top. "I went with black, because, well, I figured it was the safest option."

"Um… thank you."

"Come on, there're bathrooms downstairs where you can change." She turns around and starts walking down the hall.

I guess I'm going swimming. Shutting Luca's bedroom door behind me, I follow Holly as she guides me through this massive house. An outdoor path leads to another building. Stepping inside, I pause, stunned. The pool house isn't like anything I've ever seen. It's a tropical paradise. A large beach-entrance pool is surrounded by palm trees and other greenery with a man-made waterfall that cascades over the deepest end.

"This is beautiful," I say.

"It is. T designed it after we had Theo. Said he needed his own pool to learn how to swim. It's over the top if you ask me. But that's my husband for you." She shrugs, walking farther into what the Valentinos call their pool house but I now see is basically their own island.

"You can change in there." Holly points to a door off to one side of the room.

"Thanks," I say.

Stepping through the door, I find myself standing in yet another luxurious bathroom, and I can't help but wonder if this family does anything subtle? I place the towel and bikini on the white and gold marble countertop. Once I'm changed, I look at myself in the mirror and question how Luca's mom managed to get my size right, especially considering the swimsuit still had the price tag attached. When I walk back out, the pool is now full of people—well, women, I guess. All the men are in some meeting.

"Holy shit. Maybe it's not too late for me to turn gay." This comes from Lilah, who's staring at me from across the pool.

"Luca would kill you and take back his kidney while he was at it," Maddie says to her sister.

"Might be worth it." Lilah laughs.

"Okay, stop. You're making her uncomfortable. Ignore them, Kat," Holly scolds the sisters.

"Um, thanks," I direct to Holly. "Also, if there were a chance I'd be into girls, I'd totally choose you." I wink at Lilah, who blushes from her neck up to her cheeks.

"Holly, I swear these Valentino children get worse with each generation." Angelica walks in with Savannah and a whole tribe of kids. Luca's aunt is holding Matilda on her hip, while pushing a stroller with a baby strapped inside, followed by another little girl.

"Nonna, I gots a new suit," the girl, who I was just told is named Liliana, says proudly, doing a spin when she spots Holly.

"I see that. It's so pretty, Lily," Holly replies.

Savannah is holding on to a little boy's hand with another one in her arms. "Okay, Lilah, you've got this one," she says, passing the toddler over.

"Wait… why do I get stuck with Matteo 2.0?" Lilah complains as she smiles at the boy and picks him up anyway.

"Because you're the youngest and you can keep up with his energy," Savannah replies, stepping into the pool with the baby clutched to her chest.

Liliana jumps in after them. "I jumped all by myself, Nonna!" she squeals when Holly catches her and brings her to the surface.

"You did. You're so brave." Holly smiles at her.

Maddie climbs out of the pool and unstraps the infant from the stroller. Then Angelica sits in the shallow part with him while Matilda splashes around in the water.

I feel like an outsider. I've never had a family. I don't know how I'm supposed to act in these situations. When Liliana starts singing the chorus to one of my songs, I smile. That's something I *can* do. I turn to face her, singing along to the lyrics I know by heart. Everyone is quiet as Liliana and I belt out the tune. When it's finished, I pluck her out of Holly's arms.

"I think you might be America's next pop star, Liliana," I tell the girl.

"What's a pop star?" she asks.

"A singer."

"Oh, yeah, me can sing." She nods.

"Yes, you can," I agree.

We spend the next hour playing with the kids in the pool. By the time Luca walks into the pool house, I've relaxed and allowed myself to join in with the conversations. Which mostly consist of Lilah talking about school, the boy she's dating, and then swearing us all to secrecy. Angelica discusses her recent visit to

Italy. I've just learned that she and Neo spend half their time there and half their time here. I've never been outside of the United States. I've discussed possible overseas tours but nothing has come of it yet. I never thought I was missing out by not taking time to travel. But as I listen to Angelica's stories, then Holly bring up Australia, I'm envious of the experiences they've had.

"Bellezza, I've been looking everywhere for you," Luca says, squatting down at the edge of the pool.

"I'm sorry. Your mom asked me to come in here," I tell him.

"Zio Luc, watch me! I can be a dolphin." Liliana jumps out of my arms and swims to the edge of the pool.

"Shit, Liliana, you might have to live in the pool now that you're a dolphin," Luca tells her as he reaches down to scoop her up.

"It's pretend, silly." She rolls her eyes at him.

"Oh, thank god, I thought I was going to have to make Tilly my new favorite niece," Luca says with a relieved sigh.

"I'm still your girl, Zio Luc," Liliana says.

"Always." Luca kisses her forehead before throwing her back in the pool. Liliana lands right in front of Holly, who plucks her from the water.

"Again! Again!" Lilliana screams once she comes up and catches her breath.

"Sorry, bella, I gotta steal Katy for a bit." Luca bends down. His hands grip under my arms and he effortlessly lifts me from the pool. Placing me on my feet again, he looks me up and down with his brows furrowed. "Where the fuck did you get that suit?"

"Umm…" I take a step back and to the side. I don't do it intentionally, but his tone sets me on edge.

"I gave it to her. She looks great, don't you think, Luca?" Holly raises a brow at her son.

"Fucking too great," Luca says more softly, shaking his head. He steps closer to me. His hand cups my jaw as he leans down and his mouth grazes across my cheek. "I'm sorry. You're always safe with me, Katarina," he whispers into my ear. "Although your pussy is far from safe, because I'm about to fuck the shit out of it," he adds, and my whole face heats up. "I'm taking my girl back. Catch you all later," Luca says to his family, taking hold of my hand and pulling me out of the pool house.

I know he says I'm safe. And I'm doing my best to believe that, but I guess I'm constantly waiting for the other shoe to drop. Nothing can really be this good, can it?

As soon as we're out of the pool house, Luca leads me into a smaller building next to the one we just exited. "Where are you taking me?" I ask.

"I can't wait, bellezza. Also, there are a billion rooms and buildings on this estate, all of which we're going to christen… starting with the sauna."

I follow him into what I now know is the sauna. A large wooden bench seat wraps around the planked walls. Luca doesn't waste time. Locking the door from the inside, he then turns to me.

"Strip," he demands.

My mouth opens in shock. Is he serious? I look around the small room. "Here?"

"Yes, here," he confirms, pulling the shirt over the back of his head in that way men seem to have mastered.

My eyes are so busy taking in the sight of him I forgot he asked me to do the same. By the time his fingers reach the button on his jeans, my mouth is salivating. Dropping to my knees in front of him, I shove his hands out of the way and take over the task myself. I unzip his pants and pull them down to his knees. My fingers then hook into the waistband of his black boxer briefs as I slide them lower, freeing his rock-hard cock. It's pointing directly at me as a bead of precum leaks from its tip. Leaning in, I lick the center of the head and moan. He's delicious. I could actually do this every day, more than once a day. There is something about being on my knees, Luca's taste in my mouth, that is incredibly arousing.

"Fuck, bellezza, you look so fucking hot." Luca wraps the wet strands of my hair around his fist. "But you'd look better if you'd hurry up and put my whole cock in that fuckable little mouth of yours."

"Patience is a virtue, Luca," I tell him, as I cup his balls in one hand and wrap my other one around his cock, sliding my palm up and down a few times.

"A virtue I don't care to have," Luca grits out between clenched teeth.

"You want to fuck my mouth?" I ask him.

"You know I do." His free hand reaches for my chin, keeping my head still.

"Well, what are you waiting for?" I urge him as I drop my jaw in invitation and bring the tip of his cock level with my mouth, where I wrap my lips around it and suck.

"Fuck. Make sure you tap out if it gets to be too much," Luca warns right before he pushes his length all the way to the back of my throat. I work hard to relax my gag reflex, my eyes water, and he stills. Slowly, he pulls out and I take a huge breath through my nose right before he thrusts forward again. "Fucking gorgeous. Look at your greedy mouth taking all of my cock," he praises.

It's a contradiction of emotions. I feel dirty letting him fuck my mouth like this, while his filthy words send bolts of pleasure to my core. At the same time, as his fingers gently caress my cheek, I also feel treasured.

"I want you to swallow every fucking thing I give you, Katarina. Tell me you're going to be a good girl and swallow it all," he says, picking up his pace as he continues to thrust in and out of my mouth. I nod my head, while hollowing my cheeks and sucking as hard as I can with each motion of his hips. "Fuck, you feel good, baby. Do you like having your face fucked? Do you like choking on my cock?"

I nod again, the gesture slight with his firm hold on me. Before I know it, his movements become sporadic as his body tenses. My hand cups his balls, my finger presses against his taint, and then warm squirts of his seed shoot down my throat. I do my best to swallow it all, but there's so much I can't possibly get every last drop. Despite my best efforts, some leaks out the sides of my mouth.

Luca pulls his cock free, leans down, and swipes his thumb through the spilled cum. He then puts that thumb in my mouth. "Suck every last drop, Katarina." I do as I'm told, sucking the digit into my mouth and twirling my tongue around it. "Fucking perfect, so fucking perfect," Luca says, kissing the top of my forehead with a tenderness that's so contradictory to his dirty words.

Chapter Twenty-Eight

Luca

I'm in the kitchen, making Katarina a coffee when Pops walks in.

"You're making coffee?" he asks, looking at me like he's just witnessed his first alien abduction.

"It's not for me," I tell him.

"Right... Move out of the way. You're worse than Maddie, and that's saying something, because that girl may as well be serving you a cup of dirt," he grunts.

I lift my palms in the air and let him do his thing

with the coffee machine. "I have an away game I have to attend today."

"When did they say you'd be back on the field?" he asks.

"Another month."

"Okay."

"I need Katarina to come with me, which means I'm going to need Romeo, and either Matteo or Theo to come too."

"Sort it out with them, and let me know who's going. I'll send some extra guys with you," he says.

"What do you think is going to happen?" I ask him. I don't need to say more. My Pops knows what I mean.

"I don't know. We're either going to be extorted or whoever took that body wants something other than money." He looks at me. "Whatever it is, I'll sort it out."

"*I'll* sort it out. This is my mess to clean up."

"We're family, Luca. The very definition of family is having each other, never alone." Pops squeezes a hand on my shoulder. "Here, give her this. I'll guarantee she'll want to marry you when she thinks you can make coffee this good." He laughs.

"Pretty sure I have other talents to win her over." I smirk, exiting the room with the mug in hand. Walking back into my bedroom, I see that Katarina is still asleep, so I sit the cup on the bedside table. My fingers brush the hair out of her face. "Bellezza, wake up." I lean down and whisper into her ear, peppering kisses along her cheek.

"Mmm, Luca, it's too early," she moans.

My hand sneaks under the covers, cupping her naked breast and massaging it. "Mmm, bellezza, I need you to wake up, baby."

"Why?" she grumbles, rolling flat onto her back. The blankets slip to expose her bare chest. My fingers grip one of her nipples, tweaking it, before I lean down and wrap my mouth around the hardened peak. "Mmm, that's a better way to wake me up," she hums, arching her body off the bed.

I twirl my tongue around the nipple before I move on to the next one to pay it the same attention. She's squirming underneath me. She reaches a hand down, and her fingers slide between her wet folds as her legs fall open. Fuck, that's fucking hot. Watching her touch herself, seeing her getting herself off, as I lavish her breasts with my hands and mouth.

"Oh god. Luca!" she moans as she rubs her clit faster.

"That's it, bellezza, make yourself come. I want to watch you fall apart for me," I tell her.

Katarina's other hand lands on top of my head, pushing my mouth down onto her breast. "Don't stop," she begs.

I don't need to be told more than once. My tongue laps at one of her nipples while my hand pinches the other one. Her body is writhing. She's panting as she rubs faster and faster, her hips lifting off the bed. Closing my mouth around the pink bud, I bite down and then she detonates.

It's fucking beautiful. Breathtaking. A work of fucking art.

"Good morning." I lean over and kiss her lips as she comes down from her high.

"Morning." Her smile is shy.

"I made you coffee. Actually, Pops made the coffee, but it was my thought so I get the credit," I tell her.

"Your dad made me coffee?"

"Yeah, he was afraid you'd leave me if you had to endure my *dirt water*—his words, not mine." I shrug.

"Not even the apocalypse could make me leave you."

"Good, hold on to that thought. I'm bound to fuck up something sooner or later." I pause before adding, "I have an away game tomorrow. We're playing Cleveland. I have to fly out with the team, but I want you to take the jet. Matteo and Romeo will go with you."

"The jet?"

"The family jet."

"Of course your family has a jet," she says, rolling her eyes.

"We travel a lot. It makes sense." I leave out the part about how flying your own private jet is a must for illegal exporting. "Sooo, you'll come?" I ask her.

"I'll have Amy clear my schedule."

"Thank you." I lean down and kiss her again.

I'M on the team bus on our way to the airport. Most of the guys are quiet, earbuds in, and tuning out. Preparing for tomorrow's game in their heads. There're a lot of fucking superstitious fuckers on the team. I don't play into any of that. I think life is what you make of it. You can't control every outcome, as much as I might try to. Like, right now, I'd much rather be heading to the Valentino jet, traveling with Katarina. Instead, I'm stuck on a bus, wearing a suit I don't want to be wearing, on my way to a game I can't even fucking participate in.

Don't get me wrong, I want to be here for the team. I'm not a total ass. I just don't have my head in the fucking game at the moment. My mind is all over the place with everything that's happening.

The bus pulls up in front of the airport, and we all file out. Paparazzi flash their cameras, yelling out questions. I hear my name being called but I choose to ignore them, keeping my head down as I walked past them. Entering the airport, I sense it before I see it. Something is about to go down. I look up and am greeted by ten rifles pointed in my direction.

At least thirty officers are now circling where I've stopped. I smirk at them. "Bit much, don't you think?" I ask.

"Get on the floor. Now!" one of them yells at me.

For a brief moment, I consider refusing. I think about causing a fucking scene. Then I see her face.

Katarina. Dropping to the floor, I place my hands behind my back before they even request it. Some fucker lands on me, his knee digging into my spine. I grit my teeth. I will not show these filthy pigs an ounce of discomfort.

"Luca Valentino, you're under arrest for the murder of Aaron Madsen. You have the right to remain silent…"

I tune the officer out as he continues to read me my rights. Fuck them, the only thing I'll be doing is honoring my right to remain silent. I smile, realizing how much it's going to piss them off when I sit there with a straight face and tight lips. I've been trained to withstand far worse interrogations than whatever these fuckers can dish out. And I'm not stupid enough to say anything that will give myself up.

I'm grabbed by two officers, who flank each side of me as they pull me up to a standing position. I scan my teammates, looking for my coach. "Call my father," I tell him.

He knows exactly who and what my old man is. Fuck, everyone suspects, but not many actually know it. Coach gives a slight nod as I'm dragged out of the airport.

I LOOK at the clock on the wall. Two hours. I've been in this room for fucking two hours. My mind stuck on one person. Katarina. Does she know? What is she thinking?

An officer in a suit walks in and sits on the chair opposite me. "I hear you're implementing your right to remain silent," he says.

I look straight at him, imagining all the ways I could kill him with my bare hands... if they weren't presently cuffed to the fucking table.

The door opens and Matteo struts in. "Why the hell is my client cuffed? He's not a fucking animal. Uncuff him. Now," he orders, lowering himself onto the chair beside me. Thank fuck. Maybe now that my brother's been called in, I'll be getting out of here soon. "Don't say a word," Matteo says to me, like I need to be told.

"Your *client*..." the detective says, putting extra emphasis on the last word. "...is being charged for murder. We have every right to consider him a danger." He follows up by placing photos of a burned body in front of us. "This is Aaron Madsen. But you already know that, don't you, Mr. Valentino?" he asks, looking at me.

I don't answer him. I make sure my face is blank. Not giving anything away.

"What evidence do you have to charge him?" Matteo asks.

"Well, *this* for a start." The detective throws another photo on the table, and the moment I see it, I know I'm fucked.

It's a photo of Aaron hanging upside down from

the building… with me beside him, lighting the rope on fire.

"Bail hearing's set. We'll see you in court, Mr. Valentino. This goes without saying, but the district attorney will be requesting remand, seeing as you're an obvious flight risk."

I don't say anything as he leaves the room. Matteo pulls a pen out of his pocket, clicking the button on the top. He glances up at the camera in the corner and waits for the red light to stop flashing. They're not supposed to record attorney-client conversations. "It's amazing how small they can make jammers these days," he says, gesturing to the pen in his hand. "I'll get you out of here, Luca. It just might take a little longer than usual."

"How is she?" I ask. The only thing I care about right now is Katarina.

"Distraught, but she has us. We won't leave her alone," he promises me.

"Thank you."

"Bail is probably going to be denied. He's right. You're an obvious flight risk. So we need to come up with a defense strategy ASAP."

"I don't care what happens to me, Matteo. What I care about is her. Don't let any of this touch her."

"It can't touch her. She doesn't know anything. Right?" he asks. When I don't immediately answer him, he knows I've told her. "Fucking hell, Luca, really?" He combs a hand through his hair in irritation.

"Just make sure she's okay, Matteo, please."

"How do you know she's not the one behind those pictures?"

"She's not."

"I hope for your sake you're right." Matteo stands. "I'll see you in the courtroom. Don't say a fucking word to anyone," he reminds me for the millionth time.

Chapter Twenty-Nine

Katarina

I'm flanked by Luca's mother and father as I exit the courthouse, all three of his brothers walking just a few steps ahead of us. I feel like I've just left half of my soul behind me. I want nothing more than to run back inside, wrap my arms around him, and cling. My heart is shattering. I've never felt more helpless than I do right now. I can't help him. There's nothing I can do to get him out of there.

The paparazzi are insane, the worst I've ever seen

them. My face is covered by huge dark sunglasses and I'm letting my hair curtain my face. I don't want them to see the tears that are falling down my cheeks right now. Once I'm in the back of the car, Matteo on one side of me, Romeo on the other, and their parents in the front, I bring my knees up to my chest and sob. I don't care that Luca's family is seeing me fall apart. Romeo attempts to wrap an arm around my shoulder, but I shrug out of his hold. I don't want anyone to touch me. I can't even look at him right now and not see Luca. I recognize the very subtle differences, but he's so much like him it hurts.

"We have… to… get him out," I stutter between sobs.

"We will. I promise we will find a way to get him out," Matteo says.

I don't know where they're taking me until we pull up to the Valentino estate. "He can't stay in there, T," Holly says so quietly.

"Dolcezza, he won't. We will do whatever we have to do to get him out, trust me," Mr. Valentino assures her.

I'm not sure what I'm supposed to do. I climb out of the car and look up at the house. "I should go home," I murmur to no one in particular.

"This is home," Holly tells me, wrapping an arm around my waist and escorting me inside.

"I need a word. Come on." Matteo tilts his head towards a hall to our left. I follow him because, well, right now, he's the one who can tell me the most about Luca's case. He is the lawyer. "Sit down." He points to a sofa. And I take a seat, looking around the room. It's not one I've seen before. It's an office, a huge office. "I need you to sign some documents for me," Matteo says, pulling out a manilla folder. "But before you do, I need you to read this." He hands me an envelope with my name on it.

I quickly tear it open and read the contents.

Dear Katarina,

My bellezza. I'm sorry. You have no idea how sorry I am for putting you through this. As much as it would hurt, I will understand if you want to walk away. I never wanted to taint you with the darkness of my world.

I didn't want this.

I wanted us. I want us. We will get us. I have faith in my family's ability to get me out of here. Hopefully you can believe in that too.

Matteo is going to ask you to sign some papers. I wanted to do this differently. I wanted to give you the fairy tale you deserve. I pictured flying you to an exotic location. I pictured candlelight, flowers, dancing. I wanted to get down on one knee *and ask the question. I wanted to profess my undying love for you. I should have told you sooner. I shouldn't have been so scared to tell you that I am unquestionably, irrevocably, absolutely in love with you.*

I will understand if you don't sign the papers. We thought it was the best way to keep them from using you against me. But I get it if you don't want that for us. Just know that I will do everything in my power to protect you from this.

My heart is yours forever,
Luca

By the time I finish reading, I'm sobbing even harder. I look up at Matteo, who is waiting patiently. "What's he talking about? What is it that you need me to sign?" I ask him.

"Marriage documents," he says, handing me a manilla folder.

I open it and find a certificate of marriage, between me and Luca. It's dated for three days ago. Luca's signature is already on the document. Along with the signature of a judge and two witnesses, Romeo and Livvy. Taking the pen, I scrawl my name on the remaining line.

"What does this mean?" I ask Matteo.

"It means you just became my new favorite sister-in-law." He smirks. "And now that you're my sister, please tell me you rub elbows with Kelly Jude and can introduce us."

"I know her, but why would you want to meet her?" I ask.

"Not me, Savvy. She's obsessed."

"Oh, okay."

"We will get him out. I just need you to hold on. Don't give up on him."

"I don't get it. How is us being married going to help him?"

"It won't. It'll help you. They can't put you on the stand. They can't force you to testify against your husband." Matteo squints his eyes at me.

"All I know is that my husband is innocent, Matteo. He didn't do this. He wouldn't. Besides, I was with him that night, the *whole* night," I tell him.

Matteo tilts his head, inspecting every feature of my face. "Maybe you should have gone into acting, because if I didn't already know the truth, I would have believed that."

"I can testify that he was with me. I can be his alibi," I tell him.

"He would never let you lie for him, Kat. And you won't need to. This will go away. I'll find a way to make sure it does."

"How long until I can see him?"

"I'll take you to see him tomorrow." Matteo stands. "Are you going to be okay?" he asks me.

I nod, though it's anything but the truth. I'm not okay. I won't be okay. I lean my head back on the sofa and close my eyes. What the hell am I going to do? I just got married. I just married Luca Valentino. My phone vibrates through the pocket of my dress. I pull it out and see Zane's name on the screen.

"Hi," I say.

"Hey yourself, sugarpops. How ya holding up?" he asks.

"I'm okay," I lie.

"No, you're not."

"Okay, I'm not. But I'm trying really hard to be, Zane. I don't know what I'm supposed to do. I don't know how to help him. I want him out of there. He shouldn't be locked behind bars."

"I know. I have no doubt his family will have him out in no time. You need to focus on you though, Kat. Don't lose sight of your goals, what you've worked so hard to achieve, for a guy you just met a few weeks ago."

"He's not just a guy I met a few weeks ago, Zane. He's my husband," I tell him. The line goes silent. Eerily silent. I pull it away from my ear to check if the call cut out. It didn't. "Zane, say something."

"You married him? When?" he asks.

"A few days ago, in front of a judge."

"Why?"

239

"Because I love him. Why else would I marry him?"

"Did they force you into this marriage, Kat?"

"What? No, of course not. I love him, Zane. So much it hurts."

"Okay. I'm going to visit you. Marcia and bubs are doing really great. I can come for a few days."

"I don't need you to upend your life for me."

"I know you don't. But I want to."

"I'm not at home. I'm at the Valentino estate," I tell him.

"Well, make sure I'm on your approved visitor list, sugarpops, because I am coming to see you for myself."

"Okay."

"Are you… you don't… you're not back in that place, are you?" His voice is tentative. The place he's referring to is back when I tried to kill myself.

"No, I'm not. I'm okay. I just want him home."

"Okay, I'll see you in a few days."

The line goes dead, and before I can put my phone away, it rings again. This time, I groan when I see Liam's name flashing on the screen. "Hello," I answer it on speaker. I'm too tired to hold the phone to my ear anymore.

"Oh, Katy, thank god you're okay. Where are you? We're at your house and you're not here." Hailey's fake French accent fills the receiver.

"I'm not there. I'm a little preoccupied," I tell her.

"We need to go over the styles for the tour. We

have to finalize fittings, makeup, hair. There is much work to do, Katy," she says.

"I'm not going on tour. Cancel it all. I'm not galivanting around the country while my husband is locked up in jail." My voice raises in frustration.

"Your what? He's a guy you just met, Katarina, someone not worthy of you. Forget him. Come home. We can sort it all out. Get you back on track." This comes from Liam.

"Did you not hear me? Cancel the tour. I'm not going."

"You can't cancel, Katarina. You're contractually obligated to perform. You *will* be performing." Liam's tone is harsher than I've ever heard before.

Mr. Valentino walks into the office just in time to hear it too. He snatches the phone out of my hand. "Listen here, asshole. If my daughter says she's not performing, then she's not performing. She's not a fucking monkey for you fuckers. I want a copy of every single one of her contracts within the hour." I watch in awe as Luca's father disconnects the call and hands the phone back to me. "Does your manager speak to you like that often?" he asks, sitting in the chair opposite me, the one Matteo just left.

"No, never. I don't understand what his problem is right now."

"All contracts have an escape clause, Kat, and if they don't, I'll make sure they do. If you really don't want to go on this tour, tell me and I'll ensure you're not penalized."

"I don't want to leave Luca," I tell him.

He nods his head. "He's lucky to have found you."

"How can you say that? He's in jail because of me. If it weren't for me, he wouldn't have…" I stop my words. I won't say it. Not to a living soul.

"It's not your fault. Luca is who he is because I raised him to be that way. Whoever is behind this bull-shit will not get away with it."

"I'm really sorry I've brought so much drama into your life," I tell him, and I can already feel more tears welling in my eyes.

"Katarina, without drama, life would be boring. And trust me when I say you have not brought trouble to our doorstep. You are a breath of fresh air for my son, and for that, I'm grateful." Mr. Valentino pushes to his feet and walks over to the wet bar. "Drink?" he offers me.

I shake my head. "Thanks, but I don't drink. I think I'm going to go get changed."

Luca's father gives a slight nod of his head as I exit the office.

Chapter Thirty

Theo

It's been two fucking weeks with my little brother locked up in a cage like a fucking animal. If I could take his place, I would. In a heartbeat. I should have scoured the warehouse better that night. Made sure it was secure. I should have had some of our men surrounding the building, to ensure no other fuckers were loitering about. It's my fault Luca is behind bars right now. I should have been better. Done better.

I have to have faith in Matteo's abilities to get our brother out on a technicality, with the full force of the law behind him, because the other option, inciting a war, breaking Luca out, and stashing him away on a fucking deserted island somewhere... Yeah, Pops wasn't on board with that one.

If that's what it comes to, though, I'll do it. I will not let my baby brother rot behind bars. The whole family is reading through his case files as we speak. Somehow, Matteo managed to get an expedited trial date. Some shit about discovery and getting access to whatever evidence the cops have. Ma and Pops's dining room is currently piled up with boxes upon boxes. It's bullshit paperwork. Matteo assures us that inside one of these boxes is the piece of evidence we're looking for. Their fucking witnesses. Whoever the fuck handed my brother to the cops on a silver fucking platter. The same assholes I'm going to enjoy killing.

Looking around the room, my eyes land on Katarina, Luca's newfound wife. My new sister-in-law. I don't know her at all. I've had very few conversations with her, but I can tell she's not holding up okay. I watch as she stands and walks out of the room. I wait ten seconds, then follow her into the kitchen.

By the time I get there, she's hunched over in the middle of the room with tears falling down her face. "I'm sorry," she says, wiping her checks with the back of her hand.

"Don't be. I know everyone says you need to be

strong and all that bullshit, but it's okay to not be okay too," I tell her.

"I just feel so helpless. I only just found him and the universe is trying to take him away from me. It's not fair," she says.

"Not the universe, someone. And as soon as we find out who that *someone* is, I will take care of them. We're going to get him out of there, one way or another," I assure her with a curt nod.

"I know."

"I'm sorry I didn't protect him better. I'm sorry I didn't see this coming."

"It's not your fault, Theo," she says.

"It's my responsibility to look out for them, to make sure they stay out of trouble." I shrug.

"I've met your brothers, and that seems like an impossible task. Keeping them out of trouble? Seriously, when do you even sleep?" She laughs.

"They don't make it easy. That's for sure."

"I admire your family, the bond you all have with each other. How you all support and love one another. I've never had that. You're lucky."

"You have it now. This family is yours too, Katarina, the good and the bad," I tell her. "Come on, let's get back in there before Matteo loses his shit for us not working fast enough again."

"Thank you," Katarina says as we make our way back to the dining room.

Matteo

PRESSURE. It's something I usually thrive under. Having my little brother's freedom literally resting on my shoulders? That's an entirely different kind of pressure. This might just be the most important case I'll ever work on. And failure is not an option. Luca has to get out of there. How can I go on living my life on the outside, knowing he's locked behind bars? He was supposed to have it all.

Freedom to follow his dreams, to play pro football, to do something different from the rest of us. Something other than working for the family. I guess Valentinos really aren't destined for that. I look at Savannah, who is feeding Enzo a bottle. I want my boys to have more options than I did. I'm not sure I want them following in my footsteps. I want more for them.

Don't get me wrong, I love my fucking life. I have the woman of my dreams in my bed every night. I love working with my brothers—the dirtier the work, the better. But this? Fighting to get Luca out of jail, it's not a job I ever wanted to do.

I guess I always suspected I'd be fighting this fight for one of us. It's why I studied criminal law to begin with. I just never thought it'd be Luca. Honestly, I always assumed it'd be Theo or me. Never one of the twins.

Romeo

Worry. That's the one constant feeling I'm picking up on. It's from Luca. We've always had a connection with each other, being able to feel what the other is feeling. And right now, all I'm getting from him is worry. And not when it comes to himself. No, he's worried about *us*. Mostly about his new wife, Katarina.

I've given him as much assurance as I can, told him that I'm looking out for her. That I won't let anything happen to her. It's not the same though. I get it. If it were me, well, fuck, I'd be jumping over that ledge into insanity.

I know Luca can hold his own in there. We have guys on the inside who will have his back. I'm not concerned about his personal safety. I'm concerned about his fucking head. How he's dealing with having absolutely no control.

Matteo will get him out—that much I'm sure of. We're all busying ourselves with searching for that key witness the prosecution is hiding. I can't fucking wait to find out who the fuck thought it was a good idea to set up my brother.

Livvy gasps from the other side of the table. "Oh shit," she mumbles under her breath.

"What is it?" I ask her, already standing and making my way over to her.

Theo

As soon as I hear the gasp leave Livvy's mouth, I'm at her side and snatching the paper out of her hands before anyone else can. When I see the names scrawled across the top, the key witnesses, I turn to Katarina.

"I need the addresses of your manager and stylist, *now*," I tell her.

"W-why?" she asks.

"Because I'm about to fucking kill them." I do my

best to keep my calm. Judging by the terrified look on her face, it's not working.

"It can't be them. Why would they do this?" She shakes her head, her eyes wide.

"I don't know the reason, but it's them. Now, you need to choose, Katarina. Are you going to try to protect them? In vain, mind you, because either way, I will find them. Or are you going to be the wife my brother needs you to be?" I ask her.

"That's enough. Katarina, come with me," Pops says, placing a hand on her back and guiding her out of the room.

Chapter Thirty-One

Katarina

Mr. Valentino leads me into his office. This can't be a good thing, right? Having the boss of a mafia family lead you into their office. Especially when that family just discovered it was people connected to you who hand-delivered a murder case to the police, putting their beloved son, brother, nephew in jail. But Luca Valentino isn't just theirs. He's mine. He's my husband now, and there is no one alive who wants him out of that place more than I do. Being without him has been the hardest two weeks of my life. I don't even understand how someone can integrate themselves so deeply into my soul in such a short time.

I'm sure if I saw a shrink, they'd say I was crazy, had relationship attachment issues, or some shit like that. I don't care about what label I might fall under, because the love I have for that man far outweighs anything else life can throw at us.

"Take a seat." Mr. Valentino points to the chair directly in front of his desk.

I lower myself down, slipping my hands beneath my thighs. "If you're going to kill me, just don't let Luca ever find out it was his family," I blurt out. "I don't want him to lose what he has with you all."

Mr. Valentino's lips tip at the corner, and I swear I can see where Luca gets that killer smirk from. "We're not in the business of killing family, Katarina, and you are family." He leans back in his chair. "I dug through the contracts your manager sent over. I was hoping to have some things investigated and cleared up a bit more before I brought any of it to your attention. But due to our present circumstances..." I watch silently as he pulls open a drawer and sorts through it. He places a folder on the desk. "It appears your manager and stylist have been in a relationship for a few years," he says, before opening the folder and sliding over a photograph of Liam and Hailey... kissing.

"I don't get it... Liam can't stand Hailey." My brows furrow.

"That's not what I wanted to discuss though. It's this." He gestures to another document. "Bank records, your bank records." He hands over a statement; the number at the top is not one I've seen in a long time. It only has two zeros next to it.

"This can't be right," I say, staring down at the paper. "I'll call the bank. It has to be a mistake. I'm not broke. *I'm not.* I've worked so hard to be where I am. I have barely spent any of my money, and Liam, he makes investments for me. This is wrong." I glance up at Mr. Valentino.

"If you look at the transactions over the past year, they all lead to your manager's off-shore bank account, Katarina. He's been stealing from you for at least the duration of that time."

"No." I shake my head. "I can't be this broke." I know money isn't everything, but when you grow up not having any at all, those dollar signs mean something. They mean security.

"You are a Valentino, Katarina. I've already set up a trust in your name. You're far from broke, sweetheart," Mr. Valentino says.

"I don't want handouts. I've worked my freaking ass off for four years. How could they do this to me?"

"Money makes people greedy. It makes them do stupid things. You know we can't let them get away with what they've done. Not to you and not to Luca. It's my guess they tried to separate you from my son so their cash cow wouldn't run out. That tour you just cancelled, it was going to put two million dollars in their pockets. That's why they were so insistent on your cooperation."

"I want to go and visit Luca," I say. There is no one else I'd rather talk to right now. I pick up a Post-it note from the desk and pluck a pen from the pen holder. I know what I'm about to do is going to have two people killed. Two people I thought were my friends. Well, not friends, but I thought at the very least I could trust them. After scribbling down the address of Liam's house, though I suspect Mr. Valentino already knows it, I hand over the piece of paper. "I need to go and see Luca," I tell him again.

"I'll have Matteo take you."

THE GUARD STARTS to pat me down. What on earth they think I'm going to bring in here, I have no idea. His hands linger on my ass, and it takes everything in me not to knee him in the freaking balls. "If you don't remove your hands from my sister right the fuck now, I'll remove them from your body," Matteo growls.

The guard's face pales as he quickly pulls away. "You can go through." He waves a hand at the door.

"Thank you," I say.

"Don't thank them. They're fucking pigs," Matteo whispers to me. Walking into a meeting room, I find Luca sitting at the table, handcuffed to the metal bar. I hate seeing him like this. There's a guard in the corner of the room. I watch as Matteo gives him a nod.

"You got thirty minutes," the guard says before walking over and uncuffing Luca. He then exits the room.

"You heard him, kids. Thirty minutes," Matteo says, pulling a pen from his pocket. He clicks the top and places it in the middle of the table. "Fucking love this thing." He smiles and then proceeds to leave me and Luca alone.

We stare at each other, neither of us saying a word. Luca stands and slowly approaches me. "I fucking miss you so much, bellezza."

"Ditto." My voice is quiet, unsure. How will he feel when he learns that he's in here because of me, that people connected to *me* did this to him. "I have to tell you something," I say.

"It can wait." He tugs me closer, his palms cupping the backs of my thighs, and before I know it, he's picking me up. My legs wrap around his waist at the same time he presses me against the wall. Luca's lips slam on to mine. His tongue doesn't wait for permission before it delves in, swirling around my own. I can feel his hardness at my core and I grind down on it.

"I need you," I tell him, breaking the kiss. Reaching under my skirt, Luca pulls my panties aside, thrusting two fingers into my already-wet center. I let my head fall backwards, hitting the wall, before I lean forward and fuse my lips with his again. After pumping his fingers in and out of me a few times, Luca drops his hand. Then I feel the tip of his cock at my entrance and he slams into me. "Yes!" I moan into his mouth.

"I fucking love your pussy so fucking much," he says, pumping into me hard and fast. His movements are frantic, rushed. My legs tighten around his waist while my hands hold on to his shoulders as he effortlessly lifts me up and down on his shaft. "I want you to fucking come for me, Katarina. I want to see it. I want your pussy to choke the fuck out of my cock," he grits out between clenched teeth.

"Oh shit. Luca," I scream. My body starts to spasm, and when I feel one of his fingers at the entrance of my ass, pressing in just slightly, I explode. I think I actually see stars.

"Yes, give it all to me. This pussy is mine. All. Fucking. Mine," he says as he spills his seed inside me. "I love you so damn much."

"I love you." I grab his face and kiss him. "So much it hurts." Sliding down his body, I straighten my clothes and adjust my panties, which are now damp with a mixture of both of us.

"Come on, come sit down." Luca leads me over to the chair, taking a seat before tugging me onto his lap. "What's going on?" he asks.

"You made me promise once that no matter what I heard, I wouldn't leave you," I remind him.

"I remember."

"I need you to make the same promise to me," I say.

"Bellezza, that ring on your finger, it's never coming off. We are in this. For good."

I look down and twist the simple gold band around my finger.

"You know, the first thing I'm doing when I get out of here is buying you a ring that's worthy of you."

"I thought you said it was never coming off?" I smirk at him, then add, "I don't need a different ring, Luca. I just need you."

"And you have me. Now quit stalling. Tell me what you wanted to say."

"It was Liam and Hailey," I admit.

"What was Liam and Hailey?"

"They're the ones who handed the evidence to the police," I whisper.

"Okay."

Okay? That's all he's going to say?

"I'm really sorry. I had no idea. I didn't know. I understand if you hate me, but I'm begging you not to leave me." I turn around and straddle him, wrapping my arms around his neck. "I've officially become the stage-five clinger I never wanted to be," I murmur.

"Cling away, bellezza. I'm not going anywhere. I don't hate you. I could never hate you." Luca peppers my forehead with featherlight kisses.

"That's not all," I say.

"What else?"

"They stole all my money. I'm broke, Luca. But it's okay. I'm going to work harder, put out better songs. I'm going to make my money back."

"You're not broke. You're a fucking Valentino. Did Pops give you the trust yet?"

"He mentioned it, but I don't want your money, Luca. I already told your father I don't want a handout."

"It's not a handout. We're married. What's yours is mine, and what's mine is yours. You know, it's a good thing they found out who it was. It means my brother will be able to get me out of here sooner rather than later."

"I really hope you're right. I want you to come home. I don't like waking up without you."

"I'll be home before you know it. Promise," he says.

Chapter Thirty-Two

Luca

"What do you mean you can't find them?" I ask Matteo.

"Exactly that. They've disappeared." He shrugs, like it doesn't matter, like finding the fucking assholes who handed my ass to the cops and have been keeping me from my wife don't deserve what they have coming to them.

"It's been a week," I hiss.

"I'm aware." He smirks.

"Don't be an ass, Matteo. Luca, Theo found them yesterday. They won't be an issue anymore," Livvy says, elbowing him in the side.

Livvy has appointed herself my co-counsel, although she hasn't passed the bar yet. She wanted to wait a year after Matilda was born before she took it. Not that there's any doubt she'll pass with flying colors, probably get a better score than my brother did.

"Really? You couldn't let me have a little fun?" Matteo groans.

"Nope. My loyalty is to Romeo, and Romeo's loyalty lies with Luca before you, therefore, so does mine." She smiles sweetly at him.

"You actually have favorites? Fine, then guess what? Katarina is now my favorite sister-in-law. It was you, but not anymore," Matteo says.

"Okay, so what happens now? When the fuck can I get out of this place?" I interrupt them, because what the fuck? I don't have time for this.

"We have a hearing set for next week," Matteo says. "It's the soonest I could get you before the judge."

"Then what?"

"There is no trial without evidence. That photo the cops had of you—yeah, it's no longer you. It's now some random guy holding that lighter. And the witnesses they had? Gone." He shrugs. "I'll be motioning for a dismissal."

"And that will work?" I ask.

"It'll work. They have nothing, Luca. You just need to try to stay out of trouble for the next week," Livvy says.

"In this place? Easy." I laugh. "How's Katarina?" I ask them. I saw her yesterday, and it's already been too long.

"She's still staying with Ma and Pops," Matteo says.

"How's Ma?" I ask. I know she puts on a brave face, but I can see it in her eyes when she visits. It's hard for her. Seeing me like this. In here.

"She's the tough one, Luca. She'll be fine. And next week, this will all seem like a bad dream," Matteo says.

TWO DAYS MIGHT NOT SEEM that long, but in this hellhole, it feels like forever. I'm walking through the yard when some wannabe fucking cartel member comes at me swinging. His aim is shit. I duck to the left before my right fist hits its target. I've just crushed his motherfucking windpipe. My hand closes around his throat.

"Today is not your lucky day, motherfucker," I hiss in his face. Something drops from his hand, and when I look down, I find a shank. "Really? You thought you'd get the drop on me?" I laugh, shoving him aside. He falls to the ground, gasping for air before his whole face starts turning blue, and then nothing.

Well, fuck, so much for staying out of trouble.

"You gotta get out of here, man. Go." Kenny, one of the family's soldiers, says to me. I stare at him with furrowed brows. I'm not about to let anyone else take the fall for me. "Look, I'm already a lifer, but you... you've got a family to get home to. Go. I did this. Not you," he says. He bends down, picks up the shank, and jumps on top of the already-dead guy, stabbing him in the throat a few times.

I turn around and walk away. He's right. He's already in here for life, and not for anything he did for the family. Kenny walked in on his wife fucking his brother. He killed them both. Can't say I blame him, really. I mean, I'd never kill Katarina. But if I caught anyone else fucking her, you bet your ass I'd end them quickly. No matter who they were.

I head back to my cell. I need to fucking lie low for the next few days, survive this fucking cesspool so I can go home. I need to fucking go home.

———

"WOULD THE DEFENDANT PLEASE STAND," the judge says.

My whole family is here, in the seats right behind me. Matteo sits to my left, with Livvy beside him. The speech Matteo delivered is worthy of an award. I didn't understand half the legal jargon, but looking at the expression on the district attorney's face, I know whatever my brother said pissed him the fuck off.

"It's not often I have to dismiss a case before it even starts. However, I'm ruling in favor of the defendant. The evidence provided was not conclusive, and the defendant never should have been charged. Case dismissed. You're free to go, Mr. Valentino," the judge says to me, then turns to the prosecutor. "Don't ever waste my time with this nonsense again. Get your facts straight before you make an arrest."

I feel the weight of the world leave my shoulders. I'm free. I turn and hug Matteo. "Thank you so much. You have no idea how fucking grateful I am," I tell him.

"I will always fight for you, Luca, always," he says with a nod.

I hug Livvy. "Thank god Romeo found you, Liv. Don't tell Matteo, but you're going to make a way better lawyer," I whisper to her.

"Maybe. I'm just glad you're out."

A few minutes later, I'm escorted to my parents. My mom hugs me first, so fucking tight. "Don't ever do this to me again, Luca. I cannot live through this again," she cries into my chest.

"I'll do my best, Ma." I kiss her cheek before untangling myself from her and reaching for my father. "Thank you," I tell him.

"What are you thanking me for?" he asks.

"Everything, for taking care of Katarina when I couldn't."

"She's family, Luca. We will always take care of family. You know that," Pops says.

Romeo is next in line. "Thank god. You cannot leave me alone with all these heathens again, bro. Shit got crazy for a while there." He smiles.

"I'll keep that in mind next time I'm being charged for murder." I pat him on the back.

Theo is next. "Luca, let's not make a habit of this," he says as his arms wrap around me. That's Theo talk for: *I love you, bro.*

"Let's not," I agree. This whole time, as I've been hugging each of my family members, my eyes haven't left hers. Katarina. My wife. She steps up, and her arms wrap around my neck. "Oh my gosh, I was so freaking scared, Luca."

"Me too, bellezza, me too. I love you," I say into her ear.

"I love you."

"Let's go home." I take her hand and walk out of the courthouse, a free fucking man.

Epilogue

Katarina

6 months later

"Are you okay?" Amy asks.

"Yep, just nervous, I guess. It's been a while," I tell her.

"It's going to be like riding a bike, Katy. You'll see. You'll get out there and everything will feel like second nature."

"I hope you're right."

"You want your phone? Want to call Zane?" she asks.

"Sure, no need to break old habits now, right?" I take my cell from her hand.

"Why do you need to call Zane?" Luca scowls. He's sitting right next to me.

"Um, it's my routine. There are three things I do before a show. Calling Zane is one of them."

"I didn't take you for a superstitious person, Katarina. You think you know someone." He smiles.

"It's not superstition. It's routine," I correct him and stand. Walking to the other side of the room, I call Zane. He answers on the third ring.

"Sugarpops, how're things," he asks.

His voice has a way of setting me at ease. It's familiar; it's home. "Good, I'm about to go on stage."

"Oh, that's right. You got that concert in Central Park tonight."

"That's the one." I roll my eyes. There is no way he forgot.

"Well, break a leg—or actually, don't. Fuck, could you imagine your husband if you broke anything?" He laughs.

"It'd be unbearable." I chuckle with him.

"How's all that marital bliss holding up?"

"Blissful. How're Marcia and the kids?" I ask him.

"Why don't you ask them yourself?"

The door to the room opens, and Zane and Marcia walk in with their brood. Declan runs up to me. "Aunty Katy, Aunty Katy. I'm here!" he screams.

"You are! Like, it's really you." I pinch his little arm. "Oh, you're real too," I whisper like it's a secret.

"Daddy says you gotta sing on that big stage out there. Are you scared?" he asks me.

"No, I'm excited."

"Oh, phew, that's good," Declan says.

"I can't believe you came." I look up at Zane and Marcia. Little Katie, who will no doubt take after her namesake, is still asleep in the stroller.

"As if we'd miss it," Marcia says. "Come on, get over here. It's my turn." She pulls me in for a hug, and I find Luca's eyes over her shoulder. He did this. I know he did.

"Thank you," I whisper to him.

"Anytime," he mouths back at me with a wink.

Zane is the next one to wrap his big arms around me, lifting me off the ground with the gesture. "Shit, sugarpops, you gotta eat some more. You're as light as a fucking feather," he scolds as he lowers me back to my feet.

"Shut up." I hit his arm. I have lost weight, but not much. I don't miss Luca's assessing glare as he runs his eyes up and down the length of me. I've been working hard, rehearsing for this show for the past two months, which means I'm getting fitter, more toned. I can't help that.

"What did you say number two on your superstition list was?" Luca asks.

"Again, not superstition, routine. And I didn't tell you," I remind him.

"Humor me, bellezza. What is it?" he asks.

"I listen to *The Eminem Show* album. Usually while I'm getting my makeup applied. But I'm already done with that. So I just need to play a few songs. I have time still," I say, pulling up the album on my phone. The door opens and my phone falls to the floor. "No fucking way."

Luca stands and walks over to greet the person who just entered my dressing room. And not just any person. But the biggest lyrical genius of all time. "Thanks for coming. Let me introduce you to my wife. Katarina, this is Marshall," Luca says, coming to stand next to me. "Close your mouth, babe," he whispers in my ear with a chuckle.

I throw an elbow into his ribs. "Hi. Oh my god. It's really you," I say to Mr. Mathers.

"It's really me. I heard you were a fan," Marshall says. "I thought we could sing together before you go out there."

"Are you serious?"

"Deadly." He hands me a microphone. "I'm not sure if you know the lyrics…"

"I do," I interrupt him.

"Okay, let's sing for the moment," he says right before breaking into the lyrics of one of my favorite songs of all time. I join in at the chorus, doing my best to keep pace—it's not easy. Three songs later, and all my creative dreams of singing alongside one of the world's greats has been achieved. Thanks to Luca, my husband.

Luca

Six months ago, I was doubtful that I would ever get to have this. My life with Katarina. I didn't know if I'd ever make it out of that prison, and let's just say I'm happy to go down in history as the quickest person to ever get off a murder charge.

The week after I was released, I borrowed the family jet and took Katarina to Thailand. I gave her everything I said I wanted to do in my makeshift proposal letter. I declared my love for her, made my own vows to her. And gave her a ring worthy of being on her finger.

Apparently, the third thing on Katarina's list was to meditate for five minutes. Which I find strange, considering I've never witnessed my wife meditate. Ever. I'm not about to say anything negative about her routine, though. Even if I am convinced it's superstitious. I've played football my whole life. I know a superstition when I see one. But if it's what she needs, I'm going to make damn sure she has it. After meditating with Katarina, I watched her walk out on that stage, and the moment she was out there with the crowd cheering and calling her name, she really came alive.

I've seen her sing. I've seen her rehearse. But this right here, it's the real fucking deal. It's fucking amazing, and I make a vow to always ensure she has the opportunity to tour, to be on stage, no matter what life might throw at us.

"Thank you so much, New York. I love you all." Katarina blows a kiss to the crowd. "This next song is new, it's raw, and it releases next week. So you all are hearing it here first. It's different from my usual stuff, but I hope you love it anyway. This song means a lot to me. I wrote it when I first met my husband, Luca, who is my rock. My everything." Katarina looks to the side of the stage, right at me, and my whole world lights up.

She's worth it. Everything I lost is worth it because I still have her. I thought my life would just slot back into place when I was released from prison, and the charges were dropped. I mean, according to the state of New York, I'm an innocent man. However, according to my team managers, I'm a risk not worth taking. My contract was terminated under a morality clause, my dreams of playing pro football cut short along with it.

I'd do everything again, a million times over. These last six months, I've learned there's a lot more to life than football. Does it still sting whenever I catch a game on TV or visit the family's box at the stadium?

Fuck yes, it does. I'd jump back on the field in a heart-beat if I could.

But I've spent my free time working alongside my father and brothers. Learning the ropes. There are benefits that come with it after all. I can take whatever time off I need, and I can travel with Katarina wherever she wants to go.

The piano starts to play and her soft voice filters through the speakers.

"I'm not afraid of what's hunting me. My thunder roars, lightning cracks, but I won't flee. The storm brings out a wild love in me. A reckless faith on an uncharted sea."

I fucking love it. When she gets to the chorus, Katarina turns and looks me directly in the eye. This right here… I have everything that's important in life. She's it. She's what I was missing.

"'Cuz your reckless love never fails me. Your recklessness carries me away. Oh, your reckless love sets me free."

DO you need more of the Valentino world? Continue reading for a sneak peak at Remorseless Devilete (Izzy Valentino's Story)

Acknowledgments

First, I'd like to acknowledge you, the reader. The person who read through Luca and Katarina's book from start to end. Who lived in the Valentino world for a short period of time and become part of the family. I would not be here, continuing these amazing worlds with characters that speak to my heart and hopefully yours, without your continued support.

I'd like to thank my Patron members, who continue to keep my spirits lifted with their faith and belief in my words. Tawny, Megan, Juliet, Jenna, Monique, Kayla, Sam, Chris, Amber and Michelle. Sian, Tyler, Morgan. Thank you, thank you thank you for everything!!

My beta readers, Vicki, Amy, Melissa and Sam, you are all priceless. Shar and Xavier's journey would not be the same without you.

My content designer Assunta, you are an absolute gem!! Without you, not half as many people would know the The Valentino series, thank you for the amazing content and keeping my socials looking as fab as they do!

My editor, Kat, the one who polishes the story to make it the best it can possibly be. I could not do this without her—if I could lock her in my basement and keep her editing for me only, for the rest of her days, I would!

I have to thank Sammi B, from Sammi Bee Designs, the amazingly talented cover designer, who worked tirelessly on the beautiful covers for the Sons of Valentino.

About Kylie Kent

Kylie is a hopeless romantic with a little bit of a dark and twisted side. She loves love, no matter what form it comes in. Sweat, psychotic, stalkerish it doesn't matter as long as the story ends in a happy ending and tons of built in spice.

There is nothing she loves doing more than getting lost in a fictional world, going on adventures that only stories can take you.

Kylie loves to hear from her readers; you can reach her at: author.kylie.kent@gmail.com

For a complete reading order visit

Visit Kylie's website : www.kyliekent.com

Made in United States
Orlando, FL
26 June 2024

48322901R00153